D1756181

AMISH CHRISTMAS BRIDE: AN AMISH ROMANCE CHRISTMAS NOVEL

AMISH CHRISTMAS BOOKS #2

SAMANTHA PRICE

Copyright © 2019 by Samantha Price

All rights reserved.

No part of this book may be reproduced in any form or by any electronic or mechanical means, including information storage and retrieval systems, without written permission from the author, except for the use of brief quotations in a book review.

CHAPTER 1

JANE FRIEDERMAN LOOKED up at Mrs. Yoder's new house and couldn't believe she was back. It had been five years. Five long years of waiting for Matt Yoder to realize he loved her. Seemingly hundreds of letters had passed between them in those years, but not one of them had hinted that he saw her as anything other than a friend.

Then, out of nowhere the letter she'd been hoping and praying for had arrived.

The letter had come from Matt and the timing couldn't have been more perfect.

She'd made a vow to herself that if his letters remained as they were, still treating her as just a friend, she'd forget him—put him out of her mind completely, once and for all. In her mind, she'd given him until

Christmas. 'The letter' had arrived just six weeks prior to that date.

He asked her to return and stay at his mother's house for a couple of weeks. That was unusual but when he went on to say he had something important to ask, it could only mean one thing.

"Here's your suitcase, Ma'am."

She jumped. The driver had startled her from her thoughts. "Thank you." Her hand went into her bag to get him some money, but the taxi driver put his hand up.

"It's all been fixed, Ma'am. All paid for."

"Thank you." Matt had insisted on arranging the taxi and paying her fare.

"Do you want me to take it up to the house?" the driver asked.

"No thank you. I can manage." She hadn't brought but the one suitcase. No doubt Matt would send for the rest of her belongings once she accepted his proposal. She had no wish to return to her life in Holmes County.

When the taxi drove away, she stood looking at Matt's mother's house. She'd thought about this moment hundreds of times over the past years. Every time she'd seen it in her mind's eye, Matt was there, anxiously awaiting her arrival and then he'd rushed out of the house to greet her.

Where was Matt right now?

There was no one to take her heavy bag into the house.

Where was he?

When the front door opened, her heart skipped a beat. Then she was let down—and immediately felt guilty for it—when his mother, Sadie Yoder, stepped out. Her large frame filled the doorway and her full rosy cheeks beamed with delight.

"Jane!"

Sadie was a kindly woman, who always found something to laugh about. The perfect woman to have as a mother-in-law. Mrs. Yoder stepped through the door with outstretched arms and hurried down the porch steps to meet her. After they'd embraced, Mrs. Yoder, said, *"Denke* for coming."

"How could I not? Matt was insistent."

Sadie held her at arm's length to stare at her. "You haven't changed a bit. You're still as tall as a man and your head's still on fire." Sadie chortled.

Jane didn't know what to say. She'd been taunted all her life for having red hair, and ever since age twelve for being tall. She chose not to let it bother her now. At six foot even, she was taller than all the women she knew and most of the men. She was grateful that Matt was a good three inches taller.

She knew Sadie hadn't made her comments to be

cruel. How could Mrs. Yoder know words about her appearance would hurt her so?

"It's good to see you again. I'm so pleased you're back, Jane. I do hope you'll consider staying on."

"I'm not back permanently." That was how she was playing things for now, until Matt's proposal gave her a reason to stay.

"We'll have to see if we can persuade you to move back here."

Jane couldn't keep the smile from her face. As soon as she said yes to Matt, she'd waste no time sending her pre-written letter of resignation to her employer at the factory where she worked. She'd written the letter in the bus on the way from Ohio to Lancaster County. All she had to do was put a stamp on it and drop it in a mailbox.

"Let me take the suitcase for you. I've got a guest bedroom and it's all ready for you."

"I can take it."

"Nonsense, let me." Sadie reached for the suitcase and took it out of Jane's hand before she could utter another word. Then Sadie looped her other arm through Jane's and walked with her to the house. "It's not a very big suitcase. Don't you intend to be here for very long?"

"My plans are flexible. I've taken time off from my work, so depending on what Matt has to ask me, I can figure out how long I'll be staying. As long as that's all right with you."

"Of course it would be all right with me. I normally do what Matt wants. He's my best and brightest. He's very different from his four younger brothers. They all work with their hands as you know. Matt's always been more of a thinker, and also a planner. I knew from the start he was never meant for farm work. When he started the horse-feed business, I wasn't surprised."

"I agree." That was one of the things she liked about Matt. He was a very intelligent man and to her that only added to the attraction.

Sadie took her right to the bedroom at the end of the long rectangular home. The walls were distinctly cream-colored and Jane couldn't decide if they clashed somewhat with the bright-white and blue of the gingham curtains and the matching blue and white starburst-patterned quilt on the single bed.

"This is a nice room. So lovely and fresh, and colorful."

"Not too bright I hope." Laughter tumbled from Sadie.

"Oh no. It's just right. Perfect."

"You must be tired from the journey. Would you like to sleep—lie down and rest—before the evening meal?"

"I'm fine. Will Matt be here for dinner?" Waiting for him was painful. She was counting the seconds till he got there. She assumed he would feel the same and get to his mother's as soon as he possibly could. "Is Matt coming for dinner?" she asked again when she saw Sadie looking vaguely into the distance.

"*Nee*, he said something important came up today. Something that he has to take care of. He did say to let you know he'll collect you at 9 o'clock tomorrow morning."

Jane was disappointed. What could be more important than being here with her? Didn't he have an aching heart that longed to see her, too?

Sadie placed the suitcase on the bed. "Small bag, but you must've packed the kitchen sink. It's heavy as a newborn calf."

Jane laughed, then remembered Sadie was raised on a dairy farm. "Very much so."

"You got bricks in there?"

Jane laughed. "Not quite. I'm a good packer. I fold things very small and that way I'm able to fit more in. I'm not certain exactly how long I'll be staying. Matt gave me no idea."

"While you're getting unpacked I'll make us a cup of tea."

"That would be nice."

Out of nowhere, an enormous ginger tabby cat jumped on the bed giving Jane a fright.

"Get off, Mr. Grover."

"Oh, this is Mr. Grover? I remember him. He was only a kitten when I left."

"That's him all right."

Jane reached out and stroked him, and Mr. Grover walked closer to her and meowed. "He's adorable, and he's grown so large."

"That he has. He thinks he's the boss of this place too."

"I'd love to have a cat. I've often thought about it."

Sadie put her hands on her hips. "What's stopping you?"

In her heart, she never felt where she lived was truly her home. She never felt settled or that she belonged anywhere. "I will someday." Jane sat on the bed and Mr. Grover took an instant liking to her, smoothing up and down against her arm, looking for more pats.

"I'll fix us that hot tea."

"That'd be nice, *denke*."

As soon as Sadie left Jane alone with Mr. Grover, the cat jumped off the bed and followed his mistress from the room. Jane stretched out on the bed just for a moment. She'd waited the whole ride in the Greyhound counting down the hours until she would see Matt. Now she'd just have to keep counting. Still, *Gott* had listened to her prayers and what did a few hours matter when they had the rest of their lives in front of them?

Then Jane had an idea. What if he was busy planning her a surprise?

Perhaps it was going to be just like one of her dreams. He'd purchased a house for them and he was preparing it to show her tomorrow. Jane's heavy eyelids closed and she allowed the scene to play out in her mind. Matt would collect her at nine and then take her to the house. When she was inside, she'd ask who owned it. Then he would say it was theirs and that was when he'd ask her to marry him.

It was a romantic dream, and hopefully soon it would become her reality. Surely she deserved some grand gesture like that after waiting all these years.

With renewed energy, thinking about her new house and life as a wife, she bounded to her feet and unzipped her suitcase.

She unpacked her clothes into the chest of drawers and the wardrobe, and then she walked out to get reacquainted with her future mother-in-law. She found Sadie sitting on the couch in front of a roaring fire. On the coffee table in front of her was a large white china teapot and two over-sized cups and saucers. A large white plate was filled with cookies and on another plate was cake that resembled boiled fruit cake.

"Sit beside me, Jane, and I'll pour."

Jane did as she suggested. "How long have you lived here for, Sadie?" It felt odd to call her Sadie after calling her Mrs. Yoder for so many years, but Jane was an adult now and that was why it would feel even stranger calling her Mrs. Yoder. It was far too formal.

"I've only been here a year. Matt lives in the big house now."

"Is that so?"

"Why do you look surprised? He always loved that old place and it's not practical for me now since it's only one of me. There's only me, I should say." Sadie passed Jane a cup of hot tea.

"Denke. It's just that Matt never mentioned it in his letters. He just gave me this address when he knew I was coming, and he said this is where you live now. He made no mention of what had happened to your old *haus."* Now Jane knew Matt was not going to surprise her with a new house if he already owned the family home. Without much thought to what she was saying, Jane commented, "It's a large home for just him. There's only one of him, too."

"Matt may not be 'one' for very much longer. He's told me something about what he's planning. Ach, I shouldn't say more."

Sadie sipped her tea and Jane couldn't stop the smile forming on her lips. She'd done the right thing moving away so many years ago, she realized now. At the time, she'd done it to heal her broken heart and try to forget Matt. The last thing she expected was for him to start writing to her. It had apparently taken Matt years to realize his love for her, but better late than never.

SADIE HAD COOKED Jane a delicious roasted chicken dinner with baked vegetables and minted peas, and after they'd eaten it and cleaned up the dishes, it was late and time for bed.

As Jane changed into her nightgown, she tried to still the butterflies in her tummy. Tomorrow, she would see Matt's face for the first time in years, and also, her life would never be the same.

If Matt was planning something involving her, he had to be planning on proposing.

What else could it be?

After she pulled off her prayer *kapp* and tossed it on the end of the bed, she unpinned her hair, loosened the braiding, took out her pure boars-bristle brush—the one that used to belong to her mother—and ran it through her fine, thigh-length hair. With every stroke, she imagined what her and Matt's children would look like. Would they have his dark chocolate-brown hair and eyes, or would they have her reddish locks, green eyes and fair skin? Perhaps some would resemble him and her—a mixture of both.

With brush still in hand, she stretched her hands over her head and yawned. The day's journey had been long and Matt's mother, with her constant chatter and chortling over the smallest things, had been tiring. Still, it was nice to see Sadie again, and having a decent meal at the end of the busy day was much appreciated.

Jane laid the brush down, and turned off the gas lamp on the nightstand.

Slipping between the cool sheets, she wondered what Matt was thinking right now. As she'd done most nights in her life, she fell asleep thinking of a life where she was Matt's wife, raising their children.

CHAPTER 2

Ready well before nine the next morning, Jane was extra nervous. In her life, things had never happened the way she wanted them to and for that reason she half expected Matt to not show up at all.

She sat in the living room wearing one of her best dresses. Sadie was sitting next to her with Mr. Grover nestled firmly on her lap. The clock over the mantle told Jane it was three minutes after eight. The more often she kept looking at the minute hand, the slower it stubbornly moved.

"What is that?" Jane pointed to red and green fabric at the end of the couch.

"Christmas decorations for charity."

"They look interesting." Jane was trying to make conversation to fill the time. She stared at the tiny red jackets with dark green edges.

"Everything has to be in red and green. That's what they said."

"What is the charity?"

"I'm not even sure which one it is this time. One of the ladies is organizing it. I'm just one of the helpers, the seamstresses. I just do what I'm told."

"I'd love to help while I'm here. I left so fast that I didn't pack any of my needlework. Most nights I sit and sew."

"I'd be delighted if you would do some. I was wondering how I was going to get through it all."

Sadie pointed to two large black plastic bags in the corner of the room.

"What are they?" Jane asked. "Is that all red and green fabric?"

"That's right. Some of the ladies cut out the pieces already and I … we have to put all the pieces together."

"I'm so happy. I love having projects. I may not be here for very long, but I'm looking forward to helping all I can."

"Don't worry, the ladies and I will put you to good use while you're here."

Jane giggled, pleased now that she hadn't brought her own work.

"I hope you have a nice day today, Jane," Sadie said.

"*Denke,* I do too."

"He told me he had something important to discuss with you."

Her gaze swept to Sadie. "He did?" Jane studied Sadie's face to see if it gave any clues to what she knew of Matt's intentions.

"*Jah,* that's why you're here." Sadie wore a smug grin.

If Sadie didn't already know something, she'd guessed what was on Matt's mind. It was obvious why he wanted Jane to come all that way, but Jane was doing her best not to get her hopes up until she heard the words out of Matt's own mouth.

Jane smiled. "That's what he said to me, too. 'Something important.'"

"Soon, you'll know what it's all about and then you can both come back and tell me."

There was a definite sparkle in Sadie's eyes. There was no mistaking what Sadie thought her son was going to ask.

Jane's heart skipped a beat and then took off racing when the rumble of a horse and buggy sounded in her ears. While she sat there frozen to the spot, Sadie jumped to her feet leaving Mr. Grover to leap to the floor. Sadie looked at Jane, and then Jane stood too.

"That's him." Sadie pulled aside the heavy living room curtains.

Jane took in a sudden breath to ready herself to see him after too many long years apart. With shaky legs, Jane got herself to the front door. By this time, Sadie was also there and had pulled Jane's black coat off one of the pegs by the door.

"Don't forget this. It'll be frosty out there today by the look of the sky."

"*Denke.*"

Sadie helped Jane into her coat and then she opened the door.

When Jane stepped onto the porch, she looked up and saw Matt jumping down from the buggy. He stood staring at her for a moment while their eyes locked.

"*Gut mayrie,*" Sadie shouted in her usual booming voice.

"Morning, *Mamm.*"

"I've got things to do." Sadie announced as she patted Jane's arm. "I'll see you later, Jane." No sooner had Sadie spoken than she disappeared back into the house.

Matt walked toward Jane and she walked down the two porch steps to meet him. He had barely changed. The years had only served to make his features more manly. When he got closer, she saw the tiny lines that fanned out from the corners of his eyes.

He stretched out his arms and she didn't know what to do. As much as she wanted to hug him and be held in his arms, they'd never hugged before and she wasn't ready for it now. Not yet. She reached out her hand and he looked down and took hold of it with both hands. When she looked back into his face, she saw his lips turn upward into a smile. "You look good, Jane."

"So do you. You haven't changed a bit."

"Let's go. I'll take you back to my house where we can talk." He walked over and opened the buggy door for her.

She climbed in and waited for him as her heart pounded in her chest. When he was seated, he picked up the reins and smiled at her. "*Denke* for coming all this way."

"Of course I would. It sounded important and I'm always there for my friends." She was not going to admit her feelings until he did.

He gave a small nod, then moved his horse and buggy back down the driveway. "It is important. I think through our letters we've grown even closer since you left."

"I'd say that's true." Nervousness kept her talking. She didn't want him to know that she'd guessed he was going to propose. "While I'm here I'm hoping to see a lot of Jessica. It's been years since I've seen her and she's got two *kinner* that I've never met."

"That'll be good. I don't want to take up all your time. You should enjoy yourself while you're here."

While you're here? She analyzed those words. If they married, wouldn't she be staying here with him forever?

From the tone of his voice and his words, it

sounded more like she was only there for a vacation. She quickly berated herself for letting her mind travel to the very worst possibility.

He hasn't even said why he wants me here. I've got to be more positive. He wouldn't want me to come all this way for nothing, she told herself.

"As you can see, nothing much has changed around here since you've been gone."

She looked out at the fields they were passing. "I know. I was thinking that on the drive to your *mudder's haus* yesterday, in the car from the bus stop." A moment later, she said, "You never told me you took over your old family home."

He glanced over at her. "Didn't I mention it?"

"Nee."

He chuckled. "I've told you nearly everything else going on in my life."

"I know, and I you."

"I don't know why I didn't mention it. Perhaps I wanted to show it to you as a surprise, but there aren't many surprises when my *mudder* is around. She does like to talk."

Jane smiled. "She doesn't talk too much."

"She does. It's true." He grinned. "Anyway, I didn't want you to come all this way to talk about her. We were always close even as children and here we are still friends in our thirties."

"We were best friends right up until we were

twelve, or so, and then people were worried about us being too close."

He chuckled. "We were encouraged to keep away from each other for a few years there. Then you moved away and we started writing. They never could keep us apart, not really."

She didn't correct him, but she hadn't moved away until she was a grown woman of twenty five. He'd ignored her for those last few years before she left, when she was in her late teens and early twenties. He spoke as though she'd moved away as a young teenager.

As he chattered about times gone by, she wondered if he was driving to his home to propose to her this very day. That was how she'd always pictured it in her mind. Not exactly in his old home, but exactly which house he proposed in didn't matter. What mattered was he realized they were meant to be together, and finally he was doing something about it.

When they drove down the long driveway, the sprawling farm house appeared. It was almost as she remembered it. The only difference was, all the pretty and colorful gardens were gone.

"I've always loved this place." Jane sighed wistfully, hoping that one day soon she'd have the gardens to work on. She'd bring them back to how Sadie once had them.

"I feel the same about it, and that's why I had to

buy it when *Mamm* was talking about selling it to buy a smaller place. Come inside and I'll show you what I've done with it. There's still so much more to do. *Mamm* would never allow any of us to work on it after *Dat* died and the place fell into disrepair."

Jane nodded, wondering why Sadie would have done that.

"I didn't realize just how large it was until I started work on it," he said as he brought the horse to a halt.

They stepped down from the buggy and headed to the house. He pushed the front door open for her.

"This door was dark red or brown wasn't it?" She stepped into the house recalling he'd never once mentioned in his letters that he'd been painting. He had written mostly about their mutual friends, she realized at that moment, and what they were doing.

"It was. Nearly everything inside and out has been painted. I hope you'll like it."

The words send a thrill throughout her entire body. All she could think was that he'd fixed the place for her. "I don't know where you found the time with your horse-food business keeping you so busy." He laughed. "*Mamm* calls it my 'horse-food business.' You've been listening to her. It's a produce store."

"*Ach.* I'll remember that."

He proceeded to show her around. "I lifted up the old, gray linoleum not knowing what I'd find, but do you know these are the original timber floorboards from when the place was built in the 1800s?"

"They are beautiful."

"*Denke.* It was a chore getting rid of the glue. Someone had glued the linoleum right onto the wood."

"That would've been hard to remove."

"It was, and it took a long time because we were being careful not to damage the boards. I used the same workers to fix the barn with mortise and tenon joinery."

Jane didn't know what that was, but it sounded impressive. He continued the tour, showing her the changes he'd made.

"There are six rooms in this place, and thanks to my *vadder* there are two bathrooms so far. With some careful replanning, I could make each so that it would have its own bathroom." He rubbed his chin. "I'll let you in on a secret I've been tossing around. I could make this into a bed and breakfast."

"That's why you wanted this place, all the rooms?"

"*Nee.* I love it here, and it's my family's home where I grew up. I've been thinking about it these last couple of days. I won't need to grow crops. I could lease the land—part of it to one of my brothers. One of them is looking for land. I'd be much more suited to running a guest house than trying my hand at farming. I could even increase the guest capacity by transforming the attic into a large room, even fit in another bathroom up there."

"And, three of the bedrooms have fireplaces. Ohh, that would be so cozy. What about your horse feed business? Oh, I'm sorry, I mean your produce store."

"I can put in a manager to run it. I hardly need to be there as it is. The place practically runs itself. I can see myself playing host to all the tourists and guests who'd stay here. I'd make sure their stay was a comfortable one, and the cooking would be *wunderbaar*."

"You could use your *mudder* for the cooking."

Matt laughed. "I don't see things that way. Now, I have something important to say. Sit down with me."

"At last. I've been dying to know why I'm here."

He pointed to the couch in the corner of the living room. She sat, smoothing down her apron as she did so. He then sat down next to her, but not too close. Then he twisted to face her and she did the same, mirroring him.

"Jane, I have the utmost respect for you."

"And I feel the same about you. Even when I moved away I was so happy we came back together through our letters."

"That's right and out of anyone apart from my mother and my siblings, you know me best and it's because of that I need to ask you something very important."

This was the big moment.

A lump formed in the back of her throat and her head swam a little. If she'd been standing, she'd surely have needed to sit. Not wanting to forget any second of the next few moments, ones that she wanted to treasure for the rest of her life and tell their *kinner,* about she pulled her mind to attention. "You … you have something to ask me?"

"Jah." He smiled. "You know I do. That's why you're here."

"What is it?"

Everything inside him wanted to ask her to marry him. But, what if she said no? The word no was so final, so brutal. His best chance was sticking to his original plan. "I need your help with something very important."

Jane stared at him and blinked a couple of times. It was an unusual approach for a proposal. He wanted her help—as in—he wanted her to be his 'helpmeet?' He wanted her help with starting a marriage and then a family? "Of course I'll help you. What do you need my help with?"

"Marriage. I want your help in selecting a bride."

She replayed the words in her head. Had she heard right? The word 'marriage' had been one of the words she'd been waiting to hear, but 'selecting a bride?'

CHAPTER 3

NEVER COULD she have imagined he'd say those words to her, never at all—'selecting a bride.' They were never in her dreams. Her help with *selecting a bride?* But, she was sitting right in front of him. It didn't make sense. She could only utter … "Wh … what?"

He repeated his earlier words. "I value your opinion. I need your help with choosing a bride."

Her heart sank even further, and she tried not to let it show on her face. "I'm not sure I know what you mean." One thing she was pretty sure of—he didn't want to marry her.

He breathed out heavily and moved further back into the couch. "I've come to the age where I need to give marriage consideration. *Nee.* That's wrong. It's hard to talk about this." He coughed as though he was embarrassed.

"It's okay," she assured him. "You can tell me anything."

"I know, that's why you're here. I'm not giving marriage consideration. I've decided to do it. I need your help in selecting a bride. I want to be married by this Christmas. I've set myself a task, a goal."

A task? This time she couldn't help frowning. His approach to love and marriage seemed so cold. If he didn't want her, then didn't he know who he wanted? She wished he'd never brought her here. "Oh, I wish you'd told me all this before I got here." Jane had no interest in helping him choose her replacement.

"I'm sorry but it's something I didn't feel comfortable putting in a letter."

She stared at his handsome face. Was all hope for her gone? "How do you think I can go about selecting you a bride?" She shook her head. "I'm sorry. It's all a bit strange. I haven't been here for years and I don't know the women here all that well."

"I haven't explained things properly. There are five women. Two I like and three who are clearly … well, they've expressed an interest in …"

"I see." She nibbled on a fingernail and stared at the striped rug on the floor. Why didn't it occur to him that she might be an option? Was she that awful, that ugly, that abhorrent?

"I'm sorry. I know it's weird," he said. "Maybe I shouldn't have asked you. I just really want your help. I value your opinion so much and you know me better than anyone." He took hold of her hand. "Jane, I know I'm asking a lot, but would you do it for me?"

She stared into his dark eyes and couldn't refuse him. After a huge gulp swallowing all her hopes and dreams, she could only nod. What else was she to do?

His face lit up. "You will?"

"Jah, I'll do it." She blinked back her tears, refusing to be embarrassed.

"Denke, Jane. This process will be so much easier with you helping. It's time I married. I've left it far too long."

She forced herself to remain calm. All she wanted to do was burst into tears and get on the first Greyhound back to Ohio. "How am I to do this? Do I choose someone for you and you'll go along with whomever I name?"

"Nee. I want you to get to know these women and give me your recommendation. Of course, they'll know nothing of this. You'll be my friend who's visiting."

Once more, she looked at the striped rug and the lines moved turning into zigzags. She inhaled deeply and looked back at him. "It's a lot to take in."

"I'll forever be grateful. My *mudder* is so happy you're staying with her. You've always gotten along with her."

"Who wouldn't? She's lovely and she's always so happy."

He grimaced. "She talks a lot and some people can't take that."

"Hmm, she doesn't seem to talk too much. I don't think so. Anyway, do I know any of the candidates?"

His forehead furrowed. "Candidates?"

"Your possible future brides."

"Ah, I see. Well, you know Abigail Fisher."

There were many Fisher families in the community. The only Abigail Fisher she knew was only a young girl when she'd left for Ohio. "Rebecca and Stephen's *dochder?*"

"That's the one."

"Isn't she too young?"

"She's old enough."

Jane added up the years. Abigail was twenty one. "She's eleven years younger, as far as my math skills tell me, or even more."

"She's delightful. She makes me feel a certain way that no other woman has made me feel."

Maybe that was where she'd gone wrong. She had always been too much of a friend and that was why there was never any room for romance. Abigail had always been a pretty girl—honey colored skin, big brown eyes, and golden spirals of hair that sometimes managed to escape her prayer *kapp*. She would've grown into a beautiful woman. "And the second front runner?"

"Marcy Bright."

"I don't think I know anyone by that name."

"You don't. She moved here last year with her family. She's Abigail's cousin, closer to us in age."

Jane didn't feel any better with that news. If she was Abigail's cousin, she might be just as pretty. What chance did *she* have? "They're cousins? Keeping it in the family?"

"Not really. I'll only be choosing one of them."

"I know that. I meant … I don't know what I meant. Don't worry."

"Shall I tell you about the other three?"

Jane couldn't take anymore. "Some other time. Could you take me back to your *mudder's?* I feel a headache coming on."

He leaned over and touched her arm. "Are you ill?"

"*Jah*. I will be okay if I can lie down. I've never been a good traveler and the trip took a lot out of me."

He stood up and held her hand until she stood. Then, he guided her out of the house with his hand on her arm. "I'm so selfish, Jane. I've been so excited about you helping me with this I haven't considered your feelings."

It didn't matter what her feelings were. If he had any notion of her being his bride, he never would have chosen her for this task. "I'm happy to help if that's what you want." They continued walking toward the buggy and when they climbed in, Jane said, "I can stay as long as you want."

"Excellent because I'd like to be married by Christmas." He gave her a beaming smile and then took hold of the reins.

She wished he'd stop talking about marriage. All she wanted to do was cry. There was no other man for her, only him. Trying to keep it together, Jane pressed a fingernail into the palm of her hand. It hurt, and she was sure she was drawing blood, but it helped to stop the tears that were threatening.

Going along with her claim of a headache, she closed her eyes and tipped her head back. It hadn't been a lie about the headache. Now she was feeling an ache in her head for real.

"We're here, Jane," he whispered about fifteen minutes later.

She opened her eyes to see they were back at Sadie's house. "I'll have a lie down and I'm sure I'll feel a lot better."

"I'm coming for dinner tonight. I hope you'll be better by then."

Why was *Gott* torturing her? This was cruel. "I'm sure I will. You're not coming in now?"

"Too much to do today."

"I see. Just as long as you don't find a sixth contestant. Five is enough, I'd say."

He laughed. "I agree. Five is quite enough."

She stepped down from the buggy. "Bye, Matt."

"I'll come in with you."

She frowned. He'd just said he had too much to do. *"Nee.* I'll be okay. You go and do what you have to do."

"Bye, Jane. Have a good rest and I hope your headache's better soon. I can see you at dinner. We've got a lot of catching up to do."

"That's right. You've been keeping many things from me."

He smiled at her. "And *denke* for saying yes to this. It means such a lot."

"Of course."

"Mamm knows nothing of this yet."

"Okay. I'll keep that in mind."

As Jane walked toward the house, she saw the door swing open.

"That was fast." Sadie looked between Jane and the horse and buggy moving away.

"It was. I need a lie down if that's all right. I have a headache."

A pained expression took over Sadie's face. "Oh, Jane dear. That's awful. Do you get these often?" She raced to put her arm around Jane's shoulder and moved her into the house.

"Nee, I don't. It's just all that traveling from yesterday, I guess."

Sadie walked her into the bedroom and they both saw Mr. Grover curled up on the middle of the bed.

"Mr. Grover, out!" Sadie ordered.

Mr. Grover opened his eyes just slightly and then closed them again. Sadie then lifted him off the bed, and Mr. Grover gave a disgusted meow as he slinked out of the room.

"I've disturbed him."

"Ach, don't worry about him. The fire's on now. He'll curl up and sleep in front of that."

Once Jane was lying on the bed, Sadie put a hand on Jane's forehead. "You do feel a little hot. Can I get you anything?"

"Nee. It's okay. I just need to close my eyes for a couple of hours."

"You do that, dear." Sadie leaned over and kissed her forehead. "Call out if you need anything. I'll come back and check on you in a little while. I'll leave the door open for the warmth of the fire."

"Denke." Jane breathed deeply and let it out slowly.

When Sadie slowly backed away, Jane placed her hand over her swirling tummy. Visions of Abigail, and a girlish figure who represented Marcy, troubled her mind. How could she recommend any woman to him? The only woman she could truly see him with was herself.

A tear trickled down her cheek. Who was she kidding? Anyone would be happy to have a man like

Matt. He'd be a perfect match for any woman. No wonder there were five women who wanted to marry him—six including herself.

The only thing she could do was go away. Run away like she'd done years ago. Only this time, she'd never come back. He hadn't been romantically attracted to her years ago, and he certainly wasn't now. The only saving grace was that he didn't know how she felt. That would've been embarrassing. She could not let him know the extent of her feelings.

What excuse would she give for leaving?

She put a hand to her aching head. If only she were more attractive. No. Not even that would be likely to make a difference. When he looked at her, he never seemed to see a woman—a possible *fraa*. All he saw was his old childhood friend. The one he climbed trees with, and collected acorns and pine cones to paint to make Christmas decorations. The one who played in the tree house with him and swung from ropes and played at the edges of the creek.

Christmas had always been their favorite time of year and he was going to ruin it by marrying someone.

He was coming tonight for dinner. She'd talk privately with him and make some excuse why she couldn't do it. That was what she should've done in the first place. He could figure things out by himself.

It was too much responsibility.

She wouldn't make a good choice anyway.

No, she had to think up a better excuse. Perhaps say that she'd thought he wanted her there for a more important reason.

After all, she had left her home and her job because he'd made it sound like some kind of emergency. Now that she knew it wasn't, she should go home. Why prolong the agony? If her heart was broken now, how much more pain would it be to see Matt with someone he was going to spend the rest of his life with?

CHAPTER 4

Matt didn't know how to read the situation. Jane had seemed hesitant to help, but she eventually said she would. *Why the hesitation?* he puzzled.

His mind traveled to a possible life with Jane. Would she ever have any idea how much she inspired him? If she were willing to be by his side, they would have a great life. They could even build the bed and breakfast business together. She was quiet, but she had such a nice way with people. She'd be ideal.

Now, back in the present moment, he wasn't pleased. He'd desperately wanted to ask her to marry him just now, but there'd be that chance of rejection, and how would things be repaired once she'd said no? In any other part of his life he was bold, charged like a bull chasing a red flag, but Jane turned him into a quivering mess. He'd never heard of a woman doing that to a man. Jane certainly had that effect on him.

There'd been many times he'd made plans to visit her community under some pretext or other, just to see her. Each and every time, he'd canceled those plans in case he got there to find she was *planning* a life with someone else.

He'd dissected each and every word of her letters, looking for a hint of a man in her life. So far, there had been none. His best chance and probably his only chance of a life with Jane was to carry out the plan that Lanie had helped work out.

The plan was for Jane to see him as a popular man —wanted and valued by other women. He needed to do something to cause Jane to see him in a new light. He had to be more than the boy that she grew up with. If all went well, she would finally see him as a man. A man worthy of being her husband—a man with whom she could raise a family.

Lanie had said Jane would let him know of her feelings if she felt he was the one for her.

And, surely she would realize they were meant to be together when she was analyzing who would be the best wife for him?

It had been weeks since Lanie had helped him brainstorm the plan. Then he'd sat on it wondering and praying whether he should carry it out. Finally, he realized that if he never did anything he'd lose her one day for sure.

This way, there was at least a chance.

As soon as he'd sent the letter asking her to come, he felt better. Doing something was necessary, rather than waiting for something that might otherwise never happen.

"Is it a secret why Jane is here?" Sadie asked at the dinner table that night over a meal of asparagus and chicken pie.

Matt looked up at his mother, appearing shocked. *"Nee,* not at all."

Sadie glanced over at Jane before she looked back at Matt. "Well is anyone going to tell me? Matt?"

Matt interlaced his fingers together and swallowed hard. "I have asked Jane here to help me. You know how you're always saying that I should marry?"

"Of course. Go on." A smile lit Sadie's round face.

"Jane is going to help me do just that."

"I knew it, and I'm delighted to hear it. At long last. I thought the day would never come." She jumped up and kissed Jane and then threw her arms around Matt's neck. Then she wiped a tear from her eye. "I always knew you two would be together in the end. You both never saw it, but I did. I saw it from the beginning even when you were young. When will the wedding be?"

Matt's eyes opened wide. *"Ach nee, Mamm."*

"You've got it wrong, Sadie." Jane was embarrassed that Sadie had said all that.

Sadie's eyebrows pinched together as she turned to look at Jane. "What have I got wrong?"

Matt cleared his throat. "I have asked Jane here to help me select a bride."

"Select a bride?" Sadie screeched as she sat heavily on her chair.

"That's right. It's not as bad as it sounds."

"I can't believe my ears. Why have you done this to me? And, to Jane?"

Jane didn't want anyone feeling sorry for her. She raised her hand and lightly touched Sadie's arm. "It's quite alright. I'm willing to do it to help Matt be satisfied with the choice he made ... will make, I mean."

"This is the silliest thing I've ever heard." Sadie shook her head.

"I've always been a practical man, *Mamm*. It's a practical thing to do."

"You're right. I'm not practical, though, not when it comes to matters of the heart. I fell in love with your *vadder* and he fell for me. We didn't calculate it off some silly checklist or have our friends approve of each other." She glared at Matt with fire in her eyes. "Is that what you're doing? Are you giving Jane a checklist for each woman?"

"*Nee,* not at all. I just thought it would be something far different and a good way to choose someone suited to me. I want Jane to get to know each of the women and then make a recommendation."

"I don't know who you take after in the family, Matt, but it certainly is not me or your *vadder.*"

Matt looked down at the table and shook his head. In a quiet voice, he said, "I'm sorry if I've upset you."

"*Jah,* you have." Sadie stood and took the plates from Jane and from Matt even though they hadn't finished. Then Sadie walked the unfinished plates into the kitchen.

Jane had never seen Sadie like this.

"I've upset her," Matt whispered.

"She'll be alright. She'll see it's not such a bad idea." Jane had to say that so he wouldn't know she was devastated.

He smiled. "You understand me."

No, I don't, she thought, but she managed a smile nonetheless.

"I wouldn't do this ... I wouldn't ask anyone else apart from you, Jane."

"*Denke.* It's an honor to be asked to help you." She wished he'd asked her a very different question ... like, obviously, to marry him. How many times would this rejection be thrown so directly in her face over the next few weeks? Jane was a little bit pleased Sadie thought they'd be a good match, but that wasn't any use if Matt himself couldn't see it.

Sadie stormed back out of the kitchen and sat down again. "And how long is this process going to take? I'm sure Jane has better things to do with her time."

"It's quite alright. I'm taking time off work and I am willing to do that to help Matt out."

Matt reached over and grabbed his mother's hand. *"Mamm,* I need you to be okay with this because I want you to invite two of the ladies to dinner soon, so both you and Jane can get to know them better."

"Do I get a say in which one I like best?" Sadie asked.

Jane didn't like the sound of that. A bad situation had just become worse.

"I didn't know you'd want to be involved with it," Matt said.

"Well maybe I should have a say if Jane's having one. I know you too, don't forget."

"Okay. You can give me your opinion too, but I already knew you would." Matt smiled at his mother.

"I think it's a silly way to go about things. You should choose with your head as well as your heart."

"Many would disagree with you, *Mamm.* I am making the final choice but I will take what you both say into consideration."

"I never thought any child of mine would disagree

with that. Choosing a *fraa* shouldn't be this hard, Matt. You're making a chore of it."

"*Nee*. I'm making it easier."

Jane sat there quietly, listening. She wanted to defend Matt, but she found the whole thing just as ridiculous as Sadie did.

"Who's ready for apple pie?" Sadie asked.

"Me," Jane said with all the enthusiasm she could muster.

"*Jah,* me too, *Mamm.* I love your apple pies."

"And let's hope these ladies can cook a good apple pie. We should also be sampling their cooking."

Jane burst out laughing before she could stop herself. Then she covered her mouth and looked down. "Sorry," she mumbled, almost under her breath.

"I don't think I need to do that," Matt said. "I think all Amish women can cook, can't they?"

"*Jah,* I suppose they can," Sadie agreed, "but it wouldn't surprise me if you make both of them deliver a pie for a tasting."

Jane realized Sadie thought there were only two contenders. What would she say when she learned there were five?

"*Mamm,* you're being ridiculous."

Sadie picked up a serving spoon and shook it at him. "You're not too old for me to spank."

"I am," Matt said calmly, with a twinkle of amusement in his eyes.

Jane had never seen Sadie like this. Now, she wasn't even joking. Just when Jane considered excusing herself from the table, Matt spoke again.

"All I need you to do is have two women to dinner with you and Jane. Then you can tell me who you think would be best suited to me. Friday night or Saturday night, or even earlier, during this coming week."

"And who would they be? Marcy, I'm guessing?"

"Yes, Marcy and her cousin, Abigail."

Mamm scrunched up her face. "Abigail?"

"I know you think she's too young, but she's not."

Sadie's mouth twisted to the side. "There'd be a good ten years difference."

"And that's fine," Matt said.

"Is she even interested in you?"

"*Jah,* she is."

"So it's out of those two?"

"Actually, there are five of them," Jane said trying her best to hide her disapproval.

Sadie's mouth fell open as she continued to stare at her son. "I've never heard anything like it. But, if that's what you want to do then I'll go along with it and I'll even help you."

"*Denke, Mamm.*"

"I just hope that it doesn't blow up in your face." Sadie stood up again and went to the kitchen.

Jane half stood. "I should see if I can help."

"*Nee.* When she's like this it's best to let her be."

"Oh, do you think so?"

"I do. I should've told her sooner. She hates secrets being kept from her."

Sadie brought the pie back to the table and cut it in front of them. As she served the slices onto plates, she said, "I thought Jane was here for a very different reason."

Jane was so embarrassed she couldn't even look at Matt.

His mother spoke again, "How much will my opinion matter if it differs from Jane's? Have you thought about that?"

Matt picked up his fork. "If I'm honest, I'd rather have Jane's opinion. It's just that you like everyone, *Mamm.* Jane would have a better idea of who I like, and who would suit me. She knows me and—"

"All right, I know what you're going to say. You're not really interested in my opinion. You just want me to sit quietly at the dinner table while Jane gets to know them both."

"That would be good, *Mamm.* I know you'll like whomever Jane chooses."

"Hmm." Sadie pushed out her lips.

Once Matt had eaten dessert, he mumbled something about collecting them for the meeting tomorrow and him needing an early night, and then he left.

Sadie and Jane were still sitting at the table when Matt closed the front door behind him.

"Oh, Jane, I'm so sorry. I thought you were both going to tell me you were getting married—to each other."

"Don't be sorry for me. I have someone back home." She stretched the truth. There was Isaac who lived next door. A widower with an adorable little five-year-old girl, Rosalee. They were friends, nothing else. Why was it all the good men saw her as only friend material?

"I didn't know. You didn't say anything. Forgive me."

"There's nothing to forgive. He's a lovely man. His name's Isaac. It's not very serious between us at the moment." Jane giggled to hide her disappointment over Matt. "Isaac and I are not getting married tomorrow or anything like that. In fact, we haven't even talked about marriage, but we do like one another." She didn't want to stretch the truth too far.

Sadie's shoulders drooped as she stared at the table. "This is not turning out the way I wanted it to."

"Whatever happens will be *Gott's* will. It'll all work out in the end." As she spoke, Jane smiled through her doubts. It would work out for someone else, like it always did. She would never marry. If it couldn't be Matt, there was no point in marrying anyone. It wouldn't be fair. How could she marry another when her heart would always belong to one man? And if she didn't marry, she'd never have a child. The whole thing was so unfair.

Sadie quickly wiped a tear from her cheek, and turned to Jane. "All my *kinner* are married except for Matt. He's so good at making decisions, so why is finding a *fraa* so hard for him? He's making a chore of it. It shouldn't be this way." She turned her face upward. "His *vadder* wouldn't approve of this."

Then and there, the last speck of hope left Jane. She'd harden her heart, find Matt the woman most suited to him and then leave there forever and never return. Not even for Matt's wedding. "You go to bed, Sadie. I'll finish up in here."

"I won't hear of it. You're a guest."

"I'll be staying for a few weeks by the sounds of it. You'll wear yourself out if you don't allow me to help."

"I am a little tired."

"Go to bed." Jane stood up, and looped her arm through Sadie's. Sadie stood and Jane walked her to her bedroom. Once they were at the door, Jane let go of her arm and gave her a hug. *"Denke,* Sadie."

"What for?"

"For making this whole thing easier for me."

Sadie searched her face. "So you are in love with him?"

"I told you I have someone at home."

"But …." Sadie pushed out her lips. "Jane, are you sure you're not in love with my son?"

45

"Of course I love your son—as a friend, and I told you …"

"I know you told me about someone else. Isaac. It's just that I always thought that you and Matt would marry. Even when you went away, I was sure he would follow you and bring you back home."

That was exactly what Jane had been hoping for, but it never happened.

"All I can do is make sure I give him my best and honest opinion of who's the most suited to him. I've been away so long I don't really know any of these women any more. Abigail was just a young girl when I left. I've never even met Marcy and I'm not even sure who the other three are."

"You don't need to say anything more about Abigail. I know exactly what you mean and I agree. Do you think Marcy would suit Matt best?"

"Probably any one of them would. Matt is a *wunderbaar* man and he'd make a perfect husband."

"I know, that's what I think too. I have no idea why he's left it so long to think about marriage."

"Didn't you say he should only marry for love? Perhaps that's the answer? Maybe he hasn't gotten married yet precisely because of the whole notion of love. Now he's in his early thirties, and he's taking a different approach."

"You could be right, Jane. Age does make us view things differently."

"I just want to do a good job for him."

"You're a good friend to him, Jane. I only wish you wanted to be more."

Jane smiled at Sadie. If only she knew ... *"Gut nacht."* Jane turned and headed back to the kitchen. The last thing she wanted was to break down in front of Sadie. The woman was no fool, and Jane hoped she'd talked about Isaac enough to keep Sadie away from the truth of how much she loved her son. As Jane dried off the remainder of the dishes, she willed herself not to cry. What use would it be to marry Matt if he didn't love her the same in return? Then Jane felt sorry for the five women he was choosing between. Didn't he even know his own mind?

Jane stopped where she was and put down the dish.

She prayed then and there for *Gott* to take her love for Matt away.

If they were only friends, she could cope with what was going on—enjoy the process even.

When she opened her eyes, she felt much better.

The churning in her tummy had stopped. Hopefully, in time, the feelings for Matt would disappear as well.

CHAPTER 5

Over a breakfast of oatmeal and toast the next morning, Sadie announced,

"I've been giving it some thought. I know who the other three women are."

"You do?" Jane stared at Sadie, and noticed immediately the dark circles under her eyes. Had the poor woman been lying awake all night thinking and worrying?

"I think it's the Simpson twins. They're twenty-three, or thereabouts, and they're always gathered around him like buzzing bees. You'd think there was three of them or even four."

"Okay, with the twins that makes four ladies, and he said there were five so who could be the fifth?"

"I've been giving it a lot of thought. Lanie. Last year her husband just up and died leaving her a widow. Matt

49

might feel sorry for her. They do spend a fair bit of time together."

"That's sad. I remember she married Desmond Lapp. I know he was always sick when we were growing up. What did he die from?"

"He had a heart condition—I'd heard he had rheumatic fever when he was little, and that it damaged his heart. They both knew he might not have long, but they were both in prayer about it."

"Oh, that's so sad for her. Was Matt close with them?"

"I don't think so, not particularly, but he is friends with Lanie now and he is a protective man. I could see him wanting to look after her and her *dochder.* And, he's already as good as said he's going about this with his head and not his heart, so …"

"I see what you mean. I remember Lanie as a very quiet and shy girl. She's about three years younger than I am."

"That's my guesses for the remaining three of them. Hasn't he told you who they are yet?"

"*Nee,* but he will soon. He'll have to if he wants my help. I'm hoping he'll point them out to me at the meeting today."

"And he will be here soon to get us. Will you be ready?"

"*Jah,* I will."

"On Sundays, I leave the dishes soaking in the sink. I will wash 'em all tomorrow."

"Okay."

Since Sunday was the day of rest, the minimum of work was done, including household chores and cooking. Mostly leftovers were had, or simple meals that needed little preparation.

Just as Jane was placing the last dish into the sink, she heard the crunching sounds of the horse and buggy. "Sounds like Matt," she said to Sadie.

"Jah, that'll be him. It'll be no one else at this hour."

They both pulled on their black coats and black over-bonnets and headed out the door. Matt had already gotten out and was waiting to help them into the buggy.

Jane's stomach had resumed the dreadful churning feeling that had started when Matt had told her why she was there.

As soon as they were all in the buggy, Jane asked, "Where is the meeting today?"

"It's at the Shonebergers' house," Matt told her. "Before we get there, I have to arrange something with you, *Mamm.*"

"What is it?"

"I'd like you to invite Abigail and Marcy to have dinner with you one night soon, this week."

"I'll see."

Jane noticed the response wasn't very enthusiastic.

"Well, why don't you see if they can make it tomorrow night? As much as I'd like to, I can't keep Jane here forever. She has a life to get back to," Matt said.

"I know and I'll try to make everything happen as soon as possible."

Matt glanced over at his mother, taking his eyes off the road for a moment. "So, you'll do that today, *Mamm?*"

Sadie sighed. "Very well. I'll do that for you."

When they arrived at the house where the meeting was being hosted, Jane stepped down from the buggy and looked at the crowd gathered outside. It was heart-warming to be back in her old community seeing so many familiar faces. It brought to mind the fond memories of the days when her parents were still alive. Her brother and sister had both left the community and the Amish way of life, and she had been left alone. Now all her living Amish relatives were back in Ohio.

After Jane walked into the crowd and greeted every-one, and had been introduced to some new folk, she sat down with Sadie in the third row from the front. She had recognized Abigail and figured the woman with her was her cousin, Marcy. The two of them were seated behind her and Sadie, but who were these other three women Matt liked?

He still hadn't said.

Taking a quick look behind her, she scanned the

single women who sat in the back rows. After the meeting, she'd keep a close eye on Matt and see who approached him. That would be the easiest way, she figured.

All of a sudden, someone grabbed onto Jane's shoulders. Jane turned to see her childhood friend, Jessica, who was now married to one of Matt's brothers. Jane jumped to her feet and the two women stood there hugging with the bench seat between them. Jessica had put on a little weight, but apart from that she looked exactly the same.

"You didn't tell me you were coming," Jessica said, when they moved apart just slightly.

"I know. It was a last minute thing."

"Where are you staying?" asked Jessica.

"With Matt's *mudder,* Sadie. Your *mudder*-in-law."

"You could've stayed with me. I'm always asking you."

"I know. It's so good to see you."

"I can't wait to catch up. Can you stop by my *haus* tomorrow?"

Jane looked down at Sadie. "I don't have a horse and buggy to use. Sadie doesn't have one at all. She relies on Matt."

"We have two buggies, so I'll come and collect you and perhaps we can spend the day together."

"Part of the day. The morning maybe? I'll have to help Sadie with the dinner. We might be having guests tomorrow night. I wouldn't feel right if I wasn't there to help."

"I'll be fine, Jane," Sadie piped up.

"That's okay," Jessica answered Jane, totally ignoring Sadie. "I'll collect you tomorrow and tell you all my news." She turned slightly away from Sadie and patted her tummy and gave Jane a wink.

That meant Jessica was pregnant with her third child. Jane was pleased for her. "Where are Sally and Kate?"

"Over there. Sitting quietly for the first time in ages." Jessica pointed two rows behind them where two girls sat.

"They're adorable. I can't believe how big they are."

"Me neither. They've just turned six and four. Shall I collect you tomorrow at nine?"

"*Jah*, that would be perfect." Jane glanced down at Sadie, who'd been sitting listening into their conversation. "Will that be all right with you, Sadie? I won't stay long."

"Stay as long as you want. I'm perfectly capable of cooking the evening meal on my own."

"I know, but you won't have to. I'll be back in plenty of time." Jane hugged her friend once more as the elders began moving to the front of the room, signaling that it was time for everyone to stop talking and take their seats.

CHAPTER 6

ONCE THE MEETING WAS OVER, half of the long benches were moved back onto the specially built wagon, and in their place two long tables were moved inside for the meal. It wasn't long before the ladies filled the tables with food.

The cool climate made Jane hungrier than normal. While she was filling her plate with bite-sized pieces of meat and cheese, Matt approached.

"Has *Mamm* asked the girls for dinner yet?"

Jane had a quick look around for Sadie and saw her talking to Abigail.

"I'm not sure. She's talking to Abigail right now."

He looked where Jane had looked, saw his mother and then said, "Come here a moment." He started walking and she knew he wanted to have a private word with her.

She put a couple more things on her plate quickly, and after she grabbed a fork, followed him to the corner of the room.

"You asked me about the other girls?"

"Yes, I'll be interested to know who they are."

"See the twins over there? They're Anne and Beatrice." He nodded his head towards a group of six women. Jane looked for two women who looked alike, but they all looked very different.

"Are they identical twins?" She remembered Sadie talking about the twins.

"*Nee*, I'm sorry, I thought you knew the twins."

"I don't know any twins here. There are three sets of twins in my community back in Ohio, and ..."

"It's the two in the dark green dresses."

She saw them. They look similar enough to guess they might be sisters when she had taken a better look. "Ah, so that's them?"

"It is."

"And the other one? You said there were five? There's one I don't know about."

"The other one is Lanie."

"I know Lanie." Sadie had guessed correctly, and thanks to Sadie, Jane already knew about what had happened to Desmond, Lanie's husband. "It was very sad that her husband died from the heart condition."

"A woman like Lanie deserves happiness after all she's been through."

"I think every woman deserves happiness," Jane blurted out before she could stop herself. It wasn't that she didn't feel any sympathy for Lanie. She had the utmost sympathy for any woman who had lost her husband but it was true, what she said. Regardless of anyone's circumstances every single woman deserved a good man and a good marriage, and happiness. "I didn't mean that the way it sounded. I do feel for her with all the pain she must've gone through."

"I know. You don't have to look so worried, Jane. I probably know you better than I know myself." He chuckled. "Truth is, sometimes I don't think I know myself at all, that's why I was so desperate for your help."

It was comments like that Jane couldn't understand. Would any of these five women know him as well as she did? "I'll make my way over and talk to them as soon as I finish my food."

"You don't have to do that today."

"I might as well. After all, that's why I'm here."

"Thanks so much, Jane, you're such a good friend. I don't know what I would do without you."

"I'm happy to do it," she lied through her teeth. Now, right at this moment, she just wanted to be alone with her sorrow. "I should sit down to eat this."

He gave her a smile and she walked away, sat and concentrated on her food.

When Jane was nearly finished eating, Jessica and

her two girls sat down with her. Jane was so engrossed in talking to her friend, and to Kate and Sally, that when they'd finished, most everyone had already gone home. The men stood waiting for them to move so they could collect the benches they sat on and take the table away.

She said goodbye to Jessica and the girls and hurried over to the buggy where Sadie and Matt were waiting.

"I'm sorry, Matt," she said when they were in the buggy heading down the Shoneberger's driveway. "I was so pleased to see Jessica, and her girls that I'd never met before, that we couldn't stop talking and I had no chance to speak with the twins."

"It's okay. *Mamm* has them coming for the evening meal tomorrow night."

"Oh good. Are you coming too, Matt?"

"*Nee*. I want you to get to know them without me around."

Jane felt bad for thinking of herself. She was seeing Jessica tomorrow, so she could've excused herself today and introduced herself to the twins.

When they arrived at Sadie's house, Matt said, "Jane, can I fetch you tomorrow, around mid-morning?"

"Sure. Oh no, wait. Jessica is stopping by and taking me back to her place."

Sadie butted in, "Why don't you move your plans

for Jane to Tuesday? Then Jane can give you her report card on the twins, and tell you whether they failed or passed."

Matt frowned at her. "It's not like that, *Mamm*."

Jane was grateful for Sadie's suggestion. Even though she wanted to see Matt every day, she still had to process what he'd requested of her. "Tuesday's probably the best day. I'll be busy with Jessica in the morning and then I'll be helping prepare the dinner, and seeing you're not coming to the meal ..."

"Yeah, I get it. I can see what's going on here." He smiled. "I'm not welcome back here until Tuesday."

Sadie got out of the buggy. "Bye, Matt. You'll be missing a good meal."

"I know it. You'll have to cook a special meal for me again Tuesday night."

"I'll see what I can do, Matt."

Jane got out of the buggy too. "Bye, Matt. I'll do my best to get to know the twins."

"Good. One other thing you should know."

Jane's heart beat fast. She couldn't cope with anything else. "And what's that?"

"They don't like being called 'the twins.'"

Relief washed over Jane. "Oh. Okay. I'll try to remember that." Jane backed away and then she joined Sadie on the porch.

Sadie pushed the door open, and then closed it behind them. "I won't say more, but you know I don't like the idea. I've never even heard of anyone doing what he's doing."

"I know. It's a little odd, but I agreed to help him so I have to focus on doing a good job." Jane fixed a smile on her face. There was no way she was going to let Sadie know her true feelings for Matt.

CHAPTER 7

ON MONDAY MORNING, after a sleepless night, Matt was having more regrets about his plans. He was putting Jane through a lot of trouble for nothing. She was taking choosing a wife for him far too seriously. He'd never pictured the whole thing playing out like this. The whole thing seemed awkward now he was in the midst of it. He was starting to wish all the women hadn't agreed to helping him.

In truth, he had hoped in the middle of telling Jane about his plan, she'd reveal her own feelings for him. That certainly hadn't happened. Maybe Lanie would be right, and Jane's feelings for him would surface during the process of finding him a bride. The only bride he wanted her to find for him was herself.

The problem was, now Jane was distant to him, cold even. She'd never been like that and she'd put up a wall the moment she learned why she was here. That was how it seemed.

He arrived at Lanie's *haus* just as she was washing up the breakfast dishes. She made him a cup of coffee and he drank it at the kitchen table while she fussed around the kitchen.

"Lanie, I'm not sure I'm comfortable with all this deception with Jane."

"You're looking at it the wrong way. You want to marry Jane, right?" She pulled out the plug in the sink allowing the water to drain.

"*Jah,* it's true, but only if she feels the same about me. I was hoping she might."

"Then like I said at the start, if she's in love with you she'll forgive you when the truth comes out." She wiped her hands on a small towel. "And, she'll even see the funny side if she's anything like you … and you've told me she has a sense of humor."

"She has."

"Well, you're safe then." She sat down in front of him, and Mary-Lee came running out.

"More toast please, *Mamm?*"

"*Nee.* You've already had enough and I've washed the dishes. I'll give you more in an hour or so. Now run along and play with your toys while I talk to Mr. Yoder."

"I'm tired of my toys. I want the special ones. Please?"

Lanie got up and retrieved some brightly colored wooden blocks from the top shelf of the cupboard and passed them to Mary-Lee. "Now, make a *haus* and I'll be out to look at it soon."

"Denke." Mary-Lee took the small box of blocks from her and scurried out of the room.

Matt chuckled at the cute girl with her chubby cheeks and bright smile.

"I'm sorry about that. What were you saying?"

"I was talking about Jane and how I'm not comfortable with all this."

Lanie sat down again. "Don't worry. Somewhere along the way in this whole process, she'll realize she's the best woman for you. If she says nothing, you'll know she's not in love with you and that way she'll never know you were in love with her." If there was one thing Lanie knew it was that he had to get Jane out of his system once and for all if Matt and she herself were ever to have a future together. If Jane was in love with him, she'd certainly be upset by his request. She didn't want anyone hurt in all this, but as far as she saw it, it was either her being upset or Jane. She had a child to look out for—one that desperately needed a father—and Jane didn't.

Matt felt like a coward. Too scared he'd be rejected. Was that being unmanly? Or was it saving both Jane and him from embarrassment if she had no love for him?

Lanie continued, "She'll think she was helping out a good friend and she'll go back home feeling she's done a good deed." When he didn't say anything, she added, "It is the perfect plan. We thought it through and planned every detail of it."

He ran a hand through his hair. "Remind me what happens when I marry no one at the end of all this."

Lanie breathed in sharply. "Telling Jane, you mean, that you've chosen no one?"

"*Jah.*"

Lanie didn't even want to think about that. She wanted to be the one he chose. Even if it was all make-believe to him, she hoped he might fall in love with her at the end of it. "Just make some excuse. Think about it when and if it ever comes to that."

"*Ach.* I said I wanted to marry by Christmas." He shook his head.

"*Jah*, you had to, remember? Otherwise, this whole thing wouldn't have worked. There had to be a time limit and you had to sound urgent or she wouldn't have come."

He rubbed the side of his face. "I'm deceiving Jane and my *mudder*. Two of the most important people in the world."

"And they'll both forgive you if they ever find out."

"Did we really need five women? It seems a bit extreme."

"We had to make you seem desirable. Trust me, I'm

a woman. She'll wonder what she's missing out on if five women want you, and it'll cause her to stop and take another look at you."

"Okay. I'll take your word on that. I guess you're right. She'll have to be curious as to what these women see in me."

That was how Lanie had wanted it. It would make Jane think of him differently. Lanie was certain that Jane had always been in love with Matt and she suspected that was why she'd distanced herself from him all those years ago. Lanie's own plan was that after Matt got Jane out of his system, he'd finally truly 'see' her for the first time.

And, if nothing worked out with Jane, she'd be right there for Matt giving him her shoulder to cry on.

"Just relax, Matt. We've got a good plan going. If she loves you, she won't be able to stop herself telling you so. That's mainly why I thought there should be five so she sees you're not attached to any one particular woman."

He slowly nodded. "I guess I'm okay with the five now. I'll trust your judgement."

Lanie smiled. Everything was going nicely so far. The only thing that would ruin her future was if Jane was still in love with Matt.

Lanie couldn't wait to see what her future would hold. She had to visit Jane and find out straight from her lips how she felt about Matt. Matt had told her

Jane's plans for the day, and for Tuesday. "When you see Jane on Tuesday, why don't you suggest she spends some time with me on Wednesday? I'll collect her and bring her back to my *haus*. Better still, I could leave Mary-Lee with my *mudder,* and I could take Jane out somewhere."

"*Jah,* I think she'd like that. *Denke,* Lanie. You're a *gut* friend."

Lanie smiled. One day she hoped to be much, much more.

CHAPTER 8

THE VERY NEXT MORNING, Jane climbed into Jessica's buggy and then said hello to Sally and Kate who were in the back seat.

"Hello, Aunt Jane," Kate said. The younger, Sally, tried to repeat it, but it came out as a series of lilting sounds. Kate said it again, more slowly, and then Sally was able to copy her sister more accurately.

Jane smiled at them and then turned her attention to Jessica, and whispered so the girls wouldn't hear, "You're pregnant?"

"*Jah,* but I'm not telling anyone yet for another couple of months. The girls don't know yet. Only Luke knows."

"I'm so happy for you."

"*Denke.* I waited a long time for the third and I

thought it was never going to happen. When I forgot about it, it happened."

Even though Jane was happy for her friend, she couldn't believe they were the same age and Jessica was leaps and bounds ahead of her in life. All she had was a job in Ohio and she was renting a small *haus* from the bishop. "You're so blessed, Jessica." Jane's tone must've relayed what she'd been thinking.

"I know, but it will happen for you, just relax."

"I'm sure it will." Jane didn't want to be sad and depressed when she was visiting her friend. She needed a break from herself and a break from her normal reality.

It was half an hour later when Jane was sitting down with coffee and the girls were occupied with their wooden toys in the next room; Jessica came right to the point. "What are you doing back here, Jane? I know you haven't come to see me. I've been asking you every few months to come and stay with me. And, why are you staying with Sadie?"

"It was Matt who asked me to come back here."

"It was?" Jessica's face lit up.

"Don't get excited. It's not like that. He does want to marry, but the catch is he's not thinking of getting married to me."

"Oh, I'm so sorry, Jane. I know how you've always felt about him."

"He wants me to help him to choose someone."

"What?"

"*Jah*, it's true. He doesn't want me, he wants me to help him find a *fraa*. Obviously, a *fraa* who's not me."

Jessica stared at her blankly, letting it sink in. "You've got to be kidding."

"I'm not kidding at all. He says I know him better than anyone." The gut-wrenching feeling tore through her once more. "He took me to his house and then sat me down. You know what I thought he was going to ask me?"

"I do and why wouldn't you think that if he asked you to come here?"

Jane nodded, and couldn't keep everything bottled up any longer. "I thought he was going to ask me to marry him and what he asked me was like driving a knife through my heart." Tears filled her eyes.

"That's just awful. I'm so sorry, Jane. It's dreadful."

"Please don't tell anyone. Unless … did Luke mention anything to you?"

"*Nee*. The two brothers are close, but they don't talk about things like that."

"And I'm sure Matt wouldn't want it to get around. That's why I couldn't be with you all day today. Matt has arranged for Sadie to invite two of the women for dinner tonight. I want to be home to help Sadie prepare the meal."

"Two of the women?" Jessica's eyes bugged out. "Is, um, are there more than two of them?"

Jane sat back and told her friend the whole story from start to finish. Jessica was the only one who knew Jane was in love with Matt.

"Oh, you poor thing. You must be devastated."

"Pretty much. But what's the point of being upset? Surely if he was the one *Gott* had for me then we'd be in love and married by now. There must be someone else out there for me, don't you think so?" Jane wasn't convinced about that, but she desperately wanted the pain in her heart to go away.

"It's not for me to say. And you know your own heart. I didn't think it was a good idea for you to keep in contact with Matt. I told you that right from the start, didn't I?"

"I know, but it was hard not to write back to him with the way I feel about him and all."

Jessica shook her head. "You were dangling on a string. He was playing with you like a cat plays with a mouse. And he's still doing it. Just leave, Jane. Just leave and never speak to him again."

"I can't do that. It's too late. Maybe I should've taken your advice when I left, but I had hopes he'd write and ask me to return. He eventually did."

Jessica sighed. *"Jah,* but it wasn't what you hoped for. Would you have returned if you knew what he'd ask you?"

Jane sighed and looked down at the white handkerchief she held twisted between her fingers in her lap.

"Nee. I wouldn't. You see, I prayed about it and said to *Gott* that if Matt didn't make a move by this Christmas, I'd forget him completely. Sure, I'd still return his letters, but they'd be shorter and I'd wait for months before I returned them. So, when I saw the words—him asking me here—I convinced myself it was an answer to my prayer. You see, he made a move!"

"I can see how you'd think that. Jane, are you sure he's not brought you here because he's considering you?"

Jane huffed. "I don't want to be *considered.* I want to be the only woman he sees."

"I get you. I totally do, but if I can say something …"

Jane frowned at her friend, wondering what she was trying to say. "Go on."

"You've got to relax. Let it all go. There's got to be someone else out there for you."

"Don't you think I've told myself that one million times? But look how old I am now. What good is it to marry when I'm fifty? I'll have no *kinner.* I need to be married soon."

Jessica leaned forward and grabbed the plate of cookies and held it toward Jane. "Cookie?"

"Denke." Jane dropped the handkerchief in her lap and then reached out and took one.

"I've been trying to look on the bright side, trying to see things from a different point of view." Jane nibbled on the cookie and then put a hand over her heart. "It does hurt. He's the only man I've ever seen. No other man I've met compares. I have been looking. I haven't closed off my mind. I have been looking," she repeated.

"Hasn't anyone turned your head?"

"No. There is this one man I'm friends with, but I feel I'm just always destined to be no more than friends with the men I like. I'm sure Matt likes me, loves me even, but only as a friend. Do you know how frustrating that is for me, to love and for that love not to be returned? I might as well love a rock or a tree. *Nee,* a tree would probably show love for me more than Matt does."

"I know how you feel and I can see it now on your face."

Jane nodded. "I'll just have to get over him. And maybe this is *Gott's* way of helping me do just that. Once he's married I'll be able to get over him. I'll have to."

"You just have to get through the next couple of weeks."

"*Jah,* starting with tonight—dinner with the twins." Jane took a large bite of cookie and it fell to pieces and crumbs scattered all over her. As Jessica hurried forward to help clean the mess, Jane could only look at the cookie fragments. One thing jumped into her mind. The cookie had fallen apart, shattered into pieces, just the same as her life.

CHAPTER 9

"Now we have the twins coming for dinner tonight," Sadie said as soon as Jane walked through the door.

"I know. I've come back early to help."

"I've been thinking, Jane. If he chooses one twin, how will the other feel?"

"That's true, but I'm sure they'd rather him choose one of them than someone else."

"The twins have always liked him. That's not been a secret; it's been quite plain to see."

"He's very popular. He could probably marry any woman he wanted. In this community and any other."

Sadie nodded. "Very popular. *Gott* should've made more men."

"That definitely seems to be the case—there certainly are more women than men around here."

"That is very true, Jane. But there's not much we can do about it." Sadie smiled, rolling up her sleeves. "Let's get started on the dinner, shall we?"

Jane nodded. It was nice to be with Sadie. It reminded her of being with her own mother. Cooking together was fun.

WHEN JANE SAT down with the twins, Anne and Beatrice Simpson, she didn't know where to start. They hadn't stopped talking since they'd arrived. Each was just as annoying as the other, so how was she supposed to choose one?

The other thing was, why was Matt interested in them? She could understand why he might be interested in the other three, but the twins? That idea left her entirely baffled.

"And how long will you be here for …" the taller of the twins, Anne, spoke, and her eyes darted everywhere trying to remember her name.

"I'm Jane."

Laughter poured out from Beatrice. "Did you forget her name already? I told you one hundred times on the way here that her name's Jane."

Fingertips flew to Anne's lips. *"Jah,* I know her name is Jane I just forgot it for a moment. Forgive me, Jane. How long will you be here for, Jane?"

"A couple of weeks I think." Jane helped herself to a piece of fried chicken and then some mashed potato.

"Don't you know?"

Jane licked her lips. "Not really. I've taken vacation leave from my job and …"

"What kind of job is it?" asked Beatrice, just when Jane was about to put a forkful of chicken into her mouth.

Jane didn't want to sit there all night talking about her job. "A thoroughly uninteresting and boring one, believe me." She pushed the chicken into her mouth.

"I know what that's like, having a boring job. That's why I don't want to work—ever. I want to be someone's *fraa*. I want to get married and have *kinner* and that will be my job. Our *vadder* says we should work to bring in money before the *kinner* come along." Anne rolled her eyes.

The twins then put their heads together and giggled. Jane regretted sitting them together. There was too much noise coming from one place. If they'd been at opposite sides of the table, perhaps Jane's headache could've been more balanced.

"Enough about jobs," Beatrice said. "Tell us about Matt. How long have you known him?"

Jane swallowed and then took a mouthful of water. "I can't remember ever *not* knowing him."

Sadie interrupted, "Jane and Matthew grew up together. Her parents lived two properties down.

They've always been friends. Her parents were mine and Ralph's closest friends."

"That's right." Jane smiled at the fond memories. "That's just as I remember it too."

"Well why didn't you marry Matt?" Anne asked, as she dissected all the crispy skin off the chicken.

"Well …"

Sadie leaned forward and grabbed the bowl of mashed potato. "More potatoes for anyone?"

"Not for us thanks," Beatrice said, speaking for both of them.

"Well, Jane?" Anne asked.

"I'm not sure how I can answer that. We just didn't. We were best friends growing up but then we grew apart. It happens sometimes." Jane gulped another mouthful of water from the glass in front of her, hoping the subject would soon change.

"Jane's quite happy with her life. And she's got a man back home."

The twins stared at Sadie, and then stared at each other. Then they turned to look at Jane.

Beatrice gasped. "Do you have a man back home?"

Jane didn't know why they look so surprised. Was she that awful that they thought no man would be interested in her? She couldn't deny it now or it would look like Sadie was telling fibs. "I do. He's a very nice man."

"And he has a little girl," Sadie added.

Anne stopped chewing her food and frowned.

"His *fraa* died?" blurted Beatrice.

"Jah." Jane looked away from Beatrice because Beatrice was talking with her mouth full. "I knew her well."

"So sorry to hear that. So how did it happen?"

"You should stop talking about it, Beatrice. Can't you see that she's upset about it? A friend died and now she's involved with the husband. Of course she wouldn't want to talk about it."

Jane felt dreadful. Things weren't like that. She wasn't that good a friend of Isaac's wife, and she'd only become closer to Isaac in the last few months. Still they were friends, never anything more than that, but maybe one day many years from now something could develop between them.

Jane directed a question back to them. "Anyway, when did you two arrive in this community?"

"We're from Ephrata," Anne said.

Beatrice nodded. "We moved here with our sister when our father died."

"Oh, what do you mean, when your family died?" asked Jane.

"Nee, when our father died," Beatrice said loudly.

"Oh, I see."

"Are you hard of hearing, Jane?" Beatrice asked.

Anne said, "That happens sometimes when people get older, but you really shouldn't call attention to it, Beatrice."

"You're right. I'm sorry, Jane. I didn't mean to embarrass you."

Jane shook her head. *"Nee,* I'm not embarrassed and I'm not hard of hearing. I have excellent hearing. I just misheard what you said." And that was only because she had been speaking with her mouth full, but Jane was too polite to say that. Still, their comments only made Jane feel worse about herself. They thought she was forever single and that she was getting problems recognized as old-peoples' problems. She couldn't wait for the dinner to end, so they'd be rid of these twins.

Should she tell Matt that she didn't think either of these women suited him? What had Matt been thinking? At that moment, she felt as though she didn't know him at all. Almost anybody else in the community would've been a better choice than these two girls. Sure they were attractive with their light brown hair and their large brown eyes, but that was cancelled out by how irritating and immature they were. And if he did marry one of them, she was pretty certain the other twin would be around way too often for comfort.

Surely someone more mature like Marcy or Lanie would be a far better option for him. And besides, it was true what Sadie had said—if he chose one twin the other would be upset since they both liked him.

"It's lovely at Ephrata," said Anne, out of nowhere.

"Jah, it is nice," Jane said having fond memories of many visits there in her youth.

"We both are going to live there when we get married," Anne said.

Beatrice added, "And raise our girls together."

Anne giggled. "We're going to have twins, two sets of twins each."

"One set of girls, and then another set of boys," Beatrice said. "We're going to be pregnant at the same time and give birth around the same time."

Jane smiled. "I hope that works. That sounds delightful." She finished the last of her food, a few peas and potatoes, while the twins talked more about their childish plans for the future.

"We want the fathers of our *kinner* to be as handsome as Matt."

Anne looked over at Beatrice. "Unless one of them is Matt."

"Ach, jah."

The twins put their heads together and giggled.

As they moved on to dessert, custard tart with cream, it came out of the conversation that they both wanted to marry brothers. What was going on? All of Matt's brothers were married already.

She noticed the twin who'd said it had gotten a sharp dig in the ribs from the other twin.

Then they'd both gone quiet.

Something wasn't right.

"It's so nice to meet someone who knows Matt so well. Can you tell us any funny stories about him?"

Beatrice asked.

"I've got so many memories, we had so many happy times together growing up. I don't really have any funny stories. There is nothing I would say was funny."

Anne asked, "You didn't get into trouble or do anything naughty?"

"We probably did, but nothing that I can think of at the moment."

"Anne and I did some naughty things while we were growing up, didn't we?"

Beatrice's twin nodded enthusiastically. "We sure did. We were in trouble all the time. We were known as the terrible twins."

"That's not very nice," Jane said.

"It's quite funny really."

"Yeah, quite funny."

"Why don't you tell us about all those funny things some other time?" Sadie said, smiling awkwardly.

"Sure, we'll come again. You're such a good cook, Mrs. Yoder."

"*Denke*. I have been told that before."

"Well, it's true," Beatrice told her.

"Why don't we go to the living room and I'll bring us all out some coffee?"

"Not for me, *denke*. I don't drink coffee."

"I'll have hers then," said Beatrice.

"I'll make the coffees, Sadie. You cooked such a

lovely meal. Why don't you go to the living room with our guests?"

"*Nee*, Jane. It's quite alright. You go and I will … I won't be long."

"*Nee*. I insist. You sit down and rest with the twins."

Sadie shook her head. "Absolutely not. It's my *haus*, and you're still a guest. You do it."

Jane fixed a smile on her face. "Okay." She walked into the living room with the girls and sat down. This was her worst nightmare, but it got worse when the twins sat either side of her.

"Are you sure you don't know any stories about Matt?"

"*Jah*. We'd love to hear them."

"Tell us anything about him, anything."

"*Jah*, anything at all," the other twin said leaning even closer to her.

All Jane wanted to do was run out of the room screaming. "There's nothing to tell. Oh, I think that's Sadie needing my help in the kitchen." She bounded to her feet. "I won't be long."

"I didn't hear anything," said one twin to the other while Jane hurried away. When she walked into the kitchen, Sadie turned around to face her.

"Don't send me out there, Jane."

Jane moved closer, and whispered, "We'll both go out together as soon as the coffee's made."

"Okay and we won't offer them anything else to eat because they'll stay longer if there's more food."

Jane nodded, smiling. "Good thinking."

Jane felt wicked as she and Sadie huddled together stifling giggles.

CHAPTER 10

"WHAT DID you think about the twins?" asked Matt on Tuesday, as he drove Jane in the horse and buggy back to his house.

"Do you have a short memory?"

His mouth twisted. "What do you mean?"

"You told me they don't like to be called 'the twins,' remember?"

He laughed. "That's right. I am forgetful when it comes to some things."

"I really don't know how you want me to choose between them. They seem quite similar in their personalities. And they are very close. They even mentioned they wanted to marry brothers." She stared at him carefully to see how he'd react to that news.

His eyebrows rose. "I didn't know that."

"Perhaps you don't know them as well as you

thought." Or you haven't spent much time with them, she wanted to say.

"Maybe. I don't know what to say."

"If you want my opinion neither one of them is suitable for you. I can't see you with either twin."

"Denke, that's very helpful."

"I don't know why. You can't have seen one of them as your *fraa,* could you?"

"As I said, they expressed an interest in me and I thought I should stop and wait, and consider them."

"I can't tell you what to do, but if I were you, I would be ruling them both out."

He looked over at her and smiled. "I think you're right."

"Good, that means my job just got easier. I only have three contenders left."

He grinned at her. "I wish you'd stop calling them that."

"That's what they are and you know it."

Matt playfully shook a finger at her. It reminded her of when they were children when they were larking about.

She looked at the winding tree-lined road ahead. "Now I just have to concentrate on Lanie, Abigail, and …."

"And, Marcy."

"Ah, that's right, Marcy. Abigail's cousin, who I don't know."

"But who you'll get to know."

Trying anything she could so he wouldn't know she was in love with him, she said, "I'm flattered that you chose me to help you."

"I wouldn't trust anybody else."

"But, I'm sure you could make the decision yourself."

"I just need an objective opinion. I'll be a long time married and I don't want to make a mistake. I loved your honest comment about the twins, and once you said it, I realized how right you are. Just because they were interested in me shouldn't make me see them any differently."

For an intelligent man, he wasn't making smart decisions regarding women. "I do like the idea of turning your *haus* into a bed and breakfast, but do you think there are getting to be too many in the area?"

"I'll have to find out. If there's a call for it, I'll proceed with some plans." He shot her a quick look. "I'm pleased you like the idea."

"I do. It'll be exciting for you to have a project to work on."

"Even more so to have a woman by my side while I'm doing it. I'll correct that, while *we're* doing it—me and my future *fraa.*"

That was something she didn't want to think about. "I'm enjoying staying with Sadie. She's such good company, and so is Mr. Grover."

"*Mamm* would love having you there, but I'm sure Mr. Grover sees it as his house since he thinks he runs the place."

Jane smiled. "I've noticed that. He thinks the room where I'm staying is his. He's always in there."

"Just put him out and close the door on him."

"*Nee*. I couldn't."

"You haven't changed a bit, Jane. You still have a soft heart."

She did, only when it came to animals. She had no patience with people sometimes, especially when they were annoying twins who didn't know when to stop talking. "One day when I have a place of my own, I want a cat exactly like Mr. Grover."

"Don't you have a place already?"

"I do, but I don't own it. I'm renting it from the bishop." She knew he was wondering what happened to the money she made when she sold the farm before she moved. It was sitting in the bank. There was no point buying a house when she wasn't settled. Just because she'd lived there for years didn't mean she was settled. Her heart had to be in a place first before she bought a house. Unfortunately up until now, her heart had always been wherever Matt was.

"I hope you get everything you want, Jane."

"*Denke*, Matt. I hope so too."

He smiled. "Jane, I've arranged with Lanie that she

collect you and spend some time with you tomorrow. I hope that's all right."

"*Ach jah*. The sooner I get to know all the girls, the better. I'll look forward to it."

"Good."

"Then, when do I get to see Abigail and Marcy?"

"Later in the week. I'll have *Mamm* invite them both for dinner."

"Okay. That sounds good." Jane wondered why he'd arranged private time for her with Lanie when Abigail and Marcy didn't get one-on-one time with her. Did that mean he really preferred Lanie out of the three women who were left? It sounded that way. Marcy was the front-runner, the favorite, in Jane's mind.

THAT NIGHT, Sadie went to bed early and Jane didn't want to sit up by herself, so she headed to the bedroom. Just as she was changing into her nightgown, Mr. Grover sauntered into the room.

"Hello, there," Jane said.

He meowed at her before he jumped onto her bed. Jane recalled what she'd told Matt about the cat thinking of the room as his. That didn't matter, Jane was desperate for someone to talk with and Mr. Grover would have to do.

Jane pulled off her prayer *kapp*, tossing it onto the

bed, and then she unwound her hair that she'd braided and coiled around her head.

She picked up her brush and then sat cross-legged on the end of the bed, facing the cat, and began her nightly routine of hair brushing.

"What am I to do, Mr. Grover? It's plain that he prefers five women before me. Well, three, now that he's ruled out the twins, and they're clearly unsuitable. Why can't he see that?" She stared into the cat's eyes and he half closed them. Was she boring him with her tales of woe? That didn't deter her. He liked it there on her soft quilt; he was a captive audience. It didn't look like he was going anywhere, so listening to her was the price he'd have to pay.

"I thought things were going to be very different. I thought we'd be planning our wedding by now."

Sadie stopped still in the hallway when she heard Jane's words. She'd been about to knock on her door to ask her if she needed an extra quilt. A chilly night was headed their way. The fireplace wasn't a large one and because of that, the fire mostly went out in the early hours leaving them to wake up in a cold house.

Sadie's heart went out to Jane. She was in love with her son, and he'd broken her heart.

Still, what could she do if Matt wasn't in love with Jane? She couldn't force him to have feelings. Jane was her choice for Matt and she'd prayed off and on over the years that one day they'd be together.

Jane spoke again to Mr. Grover, "What do you care, you're only a cat and you have a perfectly lovely life with a caring owner who loves you." She tossed the brush onto the bed. "You're a very lovely cat though." She patted his soft fur. "One day if *Gott* wills it, I'll have a house of my own, Matt will be my adoring husband, and apart from all our *kinner,* we'll have a cat as lovely as you."

A knock sounded on Jane's door. "Jane, would you like another quilt, or a furry blanket? It'll be a cold night."

Jane winced, horrified. Had Sadie heard her? Just as well she'd been talking softly. *"Nee, denke,* Sadie. I'm fine. This quilt is very warm. It's like having two." Jane bit her lip.

"Okay. I'll leave a blanket here by the door just in case you get cold later on."

Jane jumped off the bed, opened the door and saw Sadie's smiling face. It didn't seem like she'd heard one single word. *"Denke."* Jane took the blanket from her. "I'm sure I'll be fine, but I'll take it just in case."

"Gut nacht, Jane."

"Sleep well, Sadie."

"I will. I always do." Sadie turned and walked away, while Jane closed the door. As soon as Jane put the blanket on the end of the bed, Mr. Grover moved himself onto it and started pawing it. "Okay, you stay there and have that one. Don't wake me in the middle of the night."

Jane then opened the bedroom door just a little in case Mr. Grover wanted to leave at some time during the night.

When she got into bed, she whispered, "I hope she didn't hear me." Then she closed her eyes and instead of worrying about the other women, she imagined herself happily married to Matt. If it wasn't going to happen in her real life, at least she could have things just the way she wanted them in her dreams.

CHAPTER 11

THE NEXT MORNING, Jane was in Lanie's buggy heading away from the house.

"What do you want to do today, Jane?"

"Anything you'd like to do. Where's Mary-Lee?"

"At my *mudder's*. She loves looking after her and it's a perfect arrangement for when I want free time, but I don't often want free time. I don't have anything to do because the truth is I don't have any friends so when Matt said you wanted to spend the day with me I was delighted."

"Why don't you have any friends? You grew up in the community."

"Everyone who has *kinner* Mary-Lee's age is married, and I really don't have anything in common with those women now. They don't know what it's like to lose a husband. All the other widows are so much older, and all the single women are so much younger."

"I see. That would be difficult."

"Jah, there are no women in my exact situation. It's hard. I've overlooked the differences, at least I've tried to, but my old friends don't treat me the same. I think they're scared. Scared that their husbands might die too if they're too close to me."

Jane frowned.

"I know that sounds silly, but that's how they act around me. Like they think it's contagious. The other groups … well, I think it doesn't occur to them to be my friend I suppose."

"That's hard. I didn't even think of people having problems like that."

"Well, you wouldn't. You wouldn't think of that until you were in that situation, and now I'm in that situation. Matt's been a friend to me, but because he's a man, I can't be too close with him without people talking. You know how things are?"

"I do. People do like to gossip—some people, that is."

"They do."

"Matt and I were close once, all through the years we were young children, but then we were told we were spending too much time together. We had to keep our distance by the order of the elders."

"How did you feel about that?" Lanie asked.

"I wasn't happy, but there wasn't much we could do. We were so young back then."

"That's too bad. I think things were different years ago. The oversight was far stricter than they are now."

Jane nodded in agreement. "I think so too. Well, I don't care what we do today. We can just go back to your *haus* if you like."

Lanie giggled. "I don't want to do that because I spend every day there. I'm getting quite sick of myself, my own company, and quite sick of the *haus*." Lanie laughed again, but Jane knew it was not a happy laugh. It was a frustrated one.

Jane felt so sorry for her. It couldn't have been easy to lose the man she loved when she was still so young.

"Take me anywhere you like. We could go into the farmers market and I'll get some food supplies for Sadie."

"Sure."

When they arrived at the markets, Jane took up a basket and walked along the aisles looking at the selection of fresh vegetables.

"I know why you're spending time with me. It's okay. The others don't know, but I know Matt is choosing between us. It's hard for him, but it must be done. I'm just glad that I'm one of the ladies he's considering."

"You don't mind that there are four more?" Jane picked up a lemon figuring she'd make a lemon tart.

"Four?"

Jane let the lemon fall from her fingers. It landed back with the others. "Oh, I'm sorry I thought you knew."

Lanie laughed. "I'm just kidding. I couldn't resist it. You should've seen your face."

Jane gave a little laugh of relief. "I thought I'd put my foot in it. So, you're the only one who knows what's really going on?"

"That's right. Matt and I have become very close over the past few months."

Jane pushed her worries from her mind and placed six lemons in her basket. Matt had never mentioned Lanie, or any of the women in his letters. Exactly how close had Lanie become with Matt? It seemed like *she* didn't know him at all anymore. In a daze, Jane filled her basket up with food and then headed to pay for it.

"What shall we do next, Jane?"

All Jane wanted to do was go back to Sadie's so she could make her lemon tart. Anything to get her mind off the pressure she was feeling. "There's a café around here somewhere. Are you hungry?"

"*Jah,* I am, but I forgot to bring money."

"My treat."

"Oh, are you sure?"

"Of course I am."

Once Jane had paid for the food, Lanie took two of

the four bags from her. "Let me take these and we can put them in the buggy now and come back."

"Good idea." On the way out through the markets, Jane wondered if she should ask a few questions of her own about Matt. Before she could, Lanie began talking again.

"I never come here. It's always so crowded, so many people."

"Where do you go?"

"My *mudder* grows fruits and vegetables, and we can and preserve them for the winter months. It's a lot of work, but it sees us through. Anything else, we get from my aunt. She has her own chickens for eggs, and buys many things in bulk lots."

"That's convenient."

"I know." They reached the buggy and then they placed the bags inside. "I feel dreadful about forgetting my money. What if we go and get it? It won't take long."

"*Nee,* that's fine. It's my treat, like I said."

"I feel awful."

"Don't. It's fine. Order anything you want. I wonder what the food's like. I'm quite hungry now."

"It's very good."

Jane stared at her wondering how she'd know.

"Oh, I never shop at the markets but I have been to that café before. You'll like it." Lanie gave her a beaming smile.

There was something that felt a little off about Lanie. Jane didn't know if she fully trusted her.

"It's so nice to have a day where I'm not sewing. Sometimes my neck and shoulders ache so much. Desmond used to massage my shoulders at the end of a big work day."

"How many days do you work?"

"I just do whatever work comes in—the repairs and the sewing jobs that come in from people I know. It covers all my bills."

It was eleven o'clock when they were seated in the café. Jane saw the time above the coffee machine. How much longer would she have to be with Lanie to be considered 'enough' time?

Jane looked through the menu and chose an open-faced sandwich of grilled cheese, ham and avocado on sourdough bread.

"I'll have the same, and an iced chocolate."

"That's easy." Jane got up and ordered at the counter. When she sat down, she said, "It is nice here."

"I told you. Wait til you taste the food."

"Lanie, what has Matt told you about me?" Jane figured she'd best get in a question or two while she could.

She noticed Lanie swallowed hard and a glazed look came over her face. "Nothing much. You're a very good friend and he's having trouble choosing a *fraa*."

"How does it make you feel to know that he's considering other women?"

"I'm fine with it. He should make a careful decision."

Jane nibbled on her thumbnail. How could any woman be fine with knowing she wasn't the only woman he was interested in? "Why are you the only one he's told about why I'm here?"

"I'm not sure. Maybe that's something you have to ask him."

Jane shot back, "I'm asking you."

"I don't know."

"If you had to guess, what would you say?"

"Maybe he knew they'd overreact. He knows I'm more calm."

"Sounds like he knows you well."

"*Jah*. He does."

Jane's coffee and Lanie's iced chocolate arrived at the table, interrupting them. "Your food won't be long," the waitress told them.

They were another hour at the café, and then they had to drive back to Lanie's house to get her money because she insisted on paying for her own meal.

Then, when Lanie eventually drove up beside Sadie's house, Sadie came right out to the buggy before Jane had a chance to get out.

"Lanie, come for dinner with us next week. Make it Monday. You and Mary-Lee, of course."

"I'd love that, Sadie. I'll look forward to it."

Jane wondered whether Matt asked his mother to invite her. She'd soon find out. Sadie would tell her.

"Good. We'll see you then."

Jane got out of the buggy. "*Denke* for a lovely day, Lanie."

"I can't remember when I had such a good time. *Denke* for coming with me." Lanie gave her a beaming smile and then waved to both Sadie and Jane as she moved her horse and buggy away.

They watched Lanie leave.

"Did you have a nice day?" Sadie asked, when Lanie was out of sight.

"I did. She's so nice. It can't be easy for her now that her husband's gone."

"I know."

"*Ach,* I'm sorry. You'd know what that's like."

"*Jah,* but she's lost him so early. *Gott* called him home and now she's got Mary-Lee to raise all on her own."

Jane nodded. Unless … someone like Matt came along and became father to Mary-Lee. "Did Matt ask you to invite her to dinner?"

"*Nee.* I thought she should come so it's fair. The others have had dinner here or will be here soon."

"That's true."

"Have you seen Matt today?" Sadie peered into her face.

"*Nee.* Is he coming for dinner?"

"He was, but he stopped by earlier to tell me he couldn't make it."

"Oh." Jane wondered what had kept him. One of the women perhaps? Since he'd now ruled out the twins, it had to be either Abigail or Marcy.

Sadie cleared her throat. "I'm sure he's working on his business tonight. He does all his own bookwork you know."

"I didn't know that."

"*Jah*, and that would keep him up late at night doing that since he always works during the day."

"I guess that's right. It would be a lot of work."

Jane gave Sadie a sideways glance as they stepped into the house. Had Sadie picked up that she was a tiny bit jealous, or that she'd been worried that he was with one of the other women?

"We're not having much for dinner tonight. We're having the same as we had last night, the leftovers."

"I love leftovers. They always taste so much better the next day." Janie's eyes went wide. *"Ach nee!"* She jumped back outside to see if she could stop Lanie.

"What's the matter, Jane?"

"I bought so much food and left it in Lanie's buggy."

Sadie laughed. "You're always enthusiastic about everything, Jane, but you're still forgetful. You haven't changed a bit."

Jane smiled.

"You didn't need to buy food. I have plenty. I'm just using the leftovers before they spoil."

Jane sighed. "Hopefully, Lanie will remember the food's in her buggy and bring it back."

"I'll make you a hot cup of tea and we can sit while you tell me all about your day."

"Ah, that does sound good."

"Now, don't forget I did invite Lanie to dinner with us for Monday night."

Jane giggled. "I know. I was there and I'll remember."

"Good. You can remember for the both of us."

Jane smiled as she took off her coat and hung it on the peg by the door while Sadie headed to the kitchen.

CHAPTER 12

LANIE GOT five minutes up the road when it dawned on her—Jane had left everything in the back of the buggy, including the drawstring bag where she kept her money. Instead of turning around and taking it directly back, she pulled the buggy off the road and jumped out.

After she had a careful look up and down the quiet country road to make sure no traffic was coming, she opened the back. The drawstring bag lay on the top of the paper shopping bags. Lanie knew it was wrong to look inside, but it could contain some answers to the many questions she had about Jane and Matt.

There could be a secret note, or some kind of letter that had passed between them.

Matt had confessed he loved Jane, but Jane acted as though he was nothing but a friend. Why wouldn't Jane love him? It didn't make sense. There had to be a logical answer since both Jane and Matt seemed such logical people.

She took a big gulp as she took hold of the bag.

I'm doing this for Mary-Lee, she told herself.

Mary-Lee needed a father. If she knew how Jane really felt, it could help her find a way into Matt's heart. Once she pulled the opening of the bag apart, all she saw was some bills neatly folded, and a few coins at the bottom

Lanie promptly pulled the strings of the bag closed.

She was none the wiser.

WHEN SADIE and Jane were seated with hot tea in the living room, Sadie had an announcement to make. "One thing I do have to tell you before I forget is that Matt has arranged for Abigail and Marcy to come for dinner on Thursday night."

"Oh! That's already tomorrow night."

"That's right. He drove me out to Marcy's place to invite them both."

"And Lanie comes to dinner on her own, next Monday. No wait, that was your idea. It was his idea for me to spend time with her alone today. He never mentioned us having dinner with Lanie, though." She stared at Sadie. "Do you think he prefers Lanie?"

Sadie took a sip of hot tea. "It's hard to say."

"It's just strange that she's the only one he didn't suggest come here for dinner."

"Not really. I think you're reading too much into it. The twins would naturally come for dinner together because they're twins. Marcy and Abigail are cousins."

"Maybe." That made Jane feel a bit better.

"He's given you an impossible task. I do have to apologize, Jane. I had no idea he was planning all this. You know why I thought you were invited here."

Jane giggled to cover up that it was the exact reason she thought she had come, too. "We'll get through it."

"*Jah,* and it'll be Christmas in no time. It's my favorite time of year."

Jane smiled. It used to be hers too as a child, but after so many lonely Christmases, she'd come to dread that time of year. It only reminded her she had no husband to love and no husband to love her in return. "He said he wants to be married by this Christmas."

Sadie frowned and set her cup onto the saucer. "That's only weeks away. I can't see it happening. Can you?"

Jane shook her head. "I haven't really given it much thought. I've been too busy trying to work out the woman best suited to him."

Mr. Grover sauntered into the room and jumped on Sadie's lap. "Mind the tea," Sadie told him.

"He must be good company for you."

"He is. Maybe you could get a cat."

Jane sighed inside. "Perhaps." Even Sadie thought she'd be single forever with only a cat to keep her company and share her home. Perhaps she *should* give up on Matt, go home and get herself a cat. At least getting a pet was something within her control. Having Matt fall in love with her was now beyond all reasonable expectations.

"So, what were your impressions of Lanie today? *Ach*, I feel dreadful asking you that, but I'm sure Matt will be asking you soon enough."

"She's very nice, just how I remembered her. It must've been so hard when her husband died."

"It was expected. He'd always been ill."

"I know, but they didn't know when the time would come. He could've lived longer. They knew all along she might be left alone to raise their *kinner*. It wasn't a surprise, I know, not really. Still, it's not easy for her. Now she's got a child to raise alone."

"She has her *mudder* to help. Every time I see Lanie lately, Mary-Lee is nowhere around. She's always got the child at her *mudder's*. Seems to me that it's Elsie who's raising the child and not Lanie." Sadie slurped her tea.

"Lanie is fortunate to have her help."

"Is it helping her, though? Shouldn't she be made to look after her own child?"

Jane took a sip of tea trying to figure out what Sadie

was getting at. "Do you know something about Lanie that I don't?"

"*Nee*, nothing. I just think that she's got it easier than people think. Everyone's feeling sad and sorry for her, but she has many advantages that other people don't. She's not too badly off."

Reading between the lines, Jane figured that Sadie didn't really like Lanie. That was surprising because Jane would've thought everyone would like Lanie with her easy-going manner and ready smile.

When they heard a buggy, Jane jumped up. "I hope that's Lanie." She opened the door to see that it was indeed Lanie. Jane continued down the steps to the buggy.

"I got halfway to my *mudder's* and I remembered you didn't get the food."

"I know. I remembered when you had barely left, but it was too late."

The two women giggled and then Jane pulled the bags out of the back. Lanie was right by her side to help her carry the bags into the house.

"Hello, Mrs. Yoder, I'm back again." Lanie giggled.

Mrs. Yoder stood. "Do you have time for hot tea? It's ready."

"*Nee, denke*. I'll have to get my *dochder* back from my *mudder*."

"Okay."

Lanie continued to the kitchen with Jane and placed the food on the table. "Is everything okay with Sadie?"

"*Jah,* why?"

"Oh nothing. I just thought she looked very tired. If it's too much for her having you stay here, you can always stay with me."

"I don't think she's tired. I'm helping her with everything as much as I can."

"I know, but you know how old people can be. They think they can do it all until they can't."

"*Denke,* for the offer, Lanie. I'll give it some serious thought. Perhaps I'll ask Sadie what she thinks."

"*Nee,* don't do that. It'll embarrass her. She'll never admit to visitors being too much for her."

"*Jah,* maybe you're right. I'll think about it."

"I'd love it if you stayed with me. It'd be so much fun."

Jane smiled, feeling good that she had the offer. Although, she'd much rather stay with Sadie. "I'll give it some thought."

"I hope you do."

CHAPTER 13

JANE WASN'T LOOKING FORWARD to dinner with Abigail and Marcy. Not if it was going to be anything like dinner with the twins. Marcy was closer to Matt's age, so Jane was certain that she was going to be the more suited between the two of them.

Sadie hadn't mentioned the two women for the entire day, not even when they were cooking for them. It was as though she was deliberately and completely trying to put them out of her mind.

For dinner, Sadie had chosen to make cabbage rolls and bologna sausage. Everything was made from scratch. For starters they'd have a traditional and hearty chicken corn soup with fresh-baked buttermilk biscuits. Dessert was to be shoo fly pies.

It was good to learn from such an experienced cook, the recipes passed down from Sadie's own great grandmother. If nothing else, Jane was learning some new recipes while she was here, as well as some interesting variations for old ones.

It wasn't long before Jane's mind traveled to a familiar negative place. What good were recipes if there was no one to cook for? No Matt to cook for, more precisely.

Jane set the table for four, trying to convince herself that the dinner mightn't be that bad. At least she might find out why Matt was interested in someone as young as Abigail. Perhaps she had a startling personality to go along with her youthful good looks.

"THAT'S THEM," Sadie said in an excited voice—the first excitement Jane had heard today—as she removed her work apron.

Sadie hurried from the kitchen while Jane stood straightening the last fork on the set table and hoping the night wouldn't be too awful. While she was listening to the voices coming in the front door, she realized she'd already made up her mind. Out of the two, she'd assumed Marcy was most suitable simply based on age. That wasn't fair, she decided. She would clear her mind of biases due to age and do her best to give each woman an equal chance.

When she saw the sausages were sizzling too much

on the stove, she turned off the gas, took the pan off the burner, and then headed out to greet the girls.

They each met her with a smile and a kiss on the cheek.

"Are we ready for dinner now, Jane?" asked Sadie as if Jane had done all the cooking.

"We are, if everyone would like to take their seats."

"We're a little late, and I'm sorry," Abigail told them as they headed into the dining room just off from the kitchen.

"That was my fault," said Marcy. "I'm always late, but I'm trying to improve."

Sadie smiled kindly. "We all have our faults. All we can do is try to better ourselves."

Although Sadie was being kind, Jane couldn't stop herself from taking a very different approach. Marcy was tardy. She knew that Matt was a very organized man. Would he cope well with a wife who was often late? Probably not.

When the two guests were seated, Jane and Sadie brought the food from the kitchen and placed it in the center of the table.

"Oh my, this looks good," Abigail said.

"It certainly does."

"*Denke.* It was a joint effort, but all Sadie's recipes."

Sadie smiled at Jane and then they closed their eyes and each said their silent prayer of thanks for the food.

Abigail opened her eyes.

Marcy giggled. *"Denke,* for cooking us a lovely meal."

"You haven't tasted it yet," said Sadie as Jane passed the bowls of food around.

"I hear you're a very good cook, Abigail," said Sadie.

Abigail giggled. "Where did you hear that from? My *mudder,* I guess."

"That's right.

"Mamm thinks I'm good at everything. I'm just average."

"Your *mudder* told me you got first prize at the *shul* open-exhibition day for your cooking. And again at the fair last year."

A smile beamed on Abigail's face. "That was for cherry pie. Anyway, you're embarrassing me."

Marcy looked at Jane, "When was the last time you saw Matt, not counting this visit?"

"I haven't seen him for quite a few years. Since I left here, I guess. We've kept in touch through our letters."

"He often talks about you." Abigail seemed to hint at more than her words alone conveyed.

"Does he?" Jane's eyebrows rose. She wanted to hear more. Why would Matt have mentioned her to Abigail?

"He talks about you all the time."

"I didn't know."

"Do you talk about him also?" Abigail fluttered her

lashes innocently, but Jane knew the question itself wasn't quite so innocent.

"To be honest, I don't think I do. That's probably because no one at my community knows him. So there probably wouldn't be much point talking about him because they wouldn't know who I was talking about."

Jane smiled on the outside, but on the inside she wished Matt had never given her the ridiculous task of finding him a wife.

"Oh this food is delicious," Abigail commented once more.

The girls were trying to be on their best behavior. It was just a simple meal of bologna and cabbage rolls.

"It's all just simple food," Sadie commented, saying exactly what Jane was thinking.

"What brings you here, Jane?" Abigail asked.

Jane coughed. She couldn't tell them why she was there. "I thought it was time to visit old friends. As I just said, I haven't been back since I left years ago. It was time."

"And do you have a boyfriend or anything?" asked Marcy.

Jane stared at Marcy. It was the kind of question she thought Abigail might ask.

"Kind of," Jane said offering an embarrassed laugh to cover the awkwardness gnawing at her tummy.

"A 'kind of' boyfriend? That sounds interesting."

"Not really. It's a developing relationship. I've

known him for quite some time." Jane shrugged her shoulders. "We'll just have to see what happens."

"Tell us about him please," asked Abigail.

"I think Jane wants to keep that to herself," Sadie said.

"Oh, I'm so sorry. I didn't mean to pry. I'm just interested in that kind of thing. I'm interested how couples get together. It seems a complete mystery to me."

"That's because you're still young," Sadie told her.

Marcy smiled. "Well, when you find out let me know, will you? I'm still waiting for someone to fall in love with me."

"Maybe someone already has fallen in love with you, Marcy, and you just don't know it yet," Abigail suggested.

"Maybe. I'll just be like Jane, I'll just wait and see."

"Good idea."

Jane didn't like where the conversation was going. She had to steer it away from love. "And what do you do for work, Marcy?"

"I work two days a week at my cousin's cafe."

"And I make candles that my cousin sells at the cafe," said Abigail.

"It's a mutual cousin," explained Marcy, "since Abigail and I are cousins, too."

"Oh, I *love* making candles," said Jane. "I haven't done that for so long. I love putting the different fragrances and the oils in the melted wax before dipping the candles."

"I'm making some tomorrow. Why don't you come to my place and we can make some that you can take home with you?"

"Oh, I couldn't do that."

"Why couldn't you?"

"I just couldn't."

"Why don't you, Jane? I don't think you have anything planned with Matt tomorrow, do you?" asked Sadie.

She had been hoping to see Matt tomorrow, but now it didn't look like it was going to happen. And she would get to know Abigail a bit better and that was the purpose of her being there. "Sure, I'd love it. That's very kind of you, *denke.*"

"I can't wait. It'll be fun."

Over dinner, Jane was slowly changing her mind. Marcy didn't seem any more mature than Abigail.

The conversation shifted back to Matt.

"So you've been spending a fair bit of time with Matt while you've been here, have you?" Marcy asked.

"Little bits and pieces."

"They were best friends growing up," Sadie told them. "They were always together. Two peas in a pod they were, except one being male and one being female. They were with each other every day until they were young teenagers."

"What happened then?" asked Marcy.

Sadie ignored the question, and continued, "You see, they only lived half a mile away. Jane was always at my *haus* or he was at hers. If either of the two of them went missing, we always knew where they could be found."

Jane had to smile. "Most of my childhood memories were the ones at your old place, out in the fields or on the rocks near the river. We had such fun."

"Sounds like you were very close," said Marcy.

"It wonders me you didn't marry him," Abigail added.

"They might have," said Sadie. "Only the elders suggested they were too close when they were in their early teens. They thought it was unhealthy that they were spending so much time with one another."

"Oh, that's sad. And so unnecessary sounding." Abigail put her fingertips to her mouth. "Oh, I didn't mean to sound like I was speaking out against the oversight."

"Nee," Marcy said. "It just sounded like you were stating your opinion, am I right?" Marcy stared at Jane and Sadie.

"That's what it sounded like to me," Sadie agreed, while Jane nodded.

"So, Jane, who became your best friend to replace Matt, all those years ago?"

"Jessica. Jessica who is now married to one of Matt's brothers."

"She's now my *dochder*-in-law."

"*Jah*, we know Jessica."

Abigail said, "I didn't know she was a good friend of yours, Jane. I remember you in the community when I was a young girl, but then you must've left."

"That's right." Jane was starting to feel very much every one of her thirty-one years.

"I remember when you left. Everyone was a little startled, but they said you moved back to where your family was originally from."

"That's right. My extended family are back there, but my two siblings who are older than me both left the community soon after our parents died."

"Oh dear! I'm sorry to hear that," said Abigail.

"Yeah, me too," added Marcy. "How did your parents die?"

"I can't remember," said Abigail, "but I recall it was sudden and they died one soon after the other."

"Ach, I'm sure Jane—"

"It's okay, Sadie. I don't mind talking about it. My *vadder* went first from pneumonia, and six months later my mother from an aneurysm. I think it was her way of being with him. They were always together, always holding hands when they sat together. We used to giggle about that when we were younger. We saw no other married couple doing that. They only did it inside the *haus* though."

"Jane's *bruder* and *schweschder* soon left the community because they said *Gott* didn't save their parents from dying young. They were stripped of their faith," Sadie told them.

"I can understand them thinking that way, but they have to know that God might have wanted them home early."

"I don't think words like that gave them much comfort." Jane said. "They had one good talk with the bishop and the elders, but that didn't stop them from leaving. I haven't heard from them since." Jane felt tears stinging behind her eyes. In a way it hurt more than her parents dying because her parents didn't have a choice in leaving her. Her brother and sister had the opportunity of making a choice and they had both just turned their backs on her and the community. Jane cleared her throat and willed the tears not to fall. On this visit, she was getting good at hiding her emotions.

That night after everyone had left and Jane was in bed, she couldn't stop crying as painful memories surfaced. She'd been left alone in their house when her brother and sister left the community. She was only seventeen, and they were nineteen and twenty. She'd gone from having a family of five, to being utterly alone in six short months. The pain and isolation she'd felt back then was like nothing else.

CHAPTER 14

JANE SPENT the next day with Abigail, making candles. She came home with a half-dozen rose scented beeswax candles and another half-dozen of lemongrass scented ones.

"How was your candle-making session?"

"Lovely, and she let me have all these. I'll share them with you."

Sadie laughed. "I have so many candles. Just give me one."

Jane put the box down on the kitchen table, and told her which ones were which. Sadie reached in and chose a rose one. "I'll light it tonight in the living room and put it in the window. Now, I have something for you."

"What is it?"

"I have a letter for you. It came today."

"A letter for me?"

"*Jah,* unless I have another Jane staying with me who has exactly the same last name." Sadie giggled.

"That's odd. The only person who has this address is the bishop."

Sadie turned the envelope over and looked at the back. "Hmm. This person could've got the address from the bishop. Know someone with the first initial of I? I for Isaac, maybe?"

"Isaac's my neighbor. Oh no, I hope there's not something wrong with my *haus,* but then I suppose since it belongs to the bishop it would be he who'd write to me."

Still holding onto the letter, Sadie said with more than a hint of mischief, "Didn't you tell me you and Isaac were a little more than friends?"

Jane felt bad for deceiving Sadie, and even worse now that her fabricated stories were coming apart at the seams. "That's right. But that doesn't mean he would write to me … necessarily. It's a very new relationship."

Sadie put the letter down on the coffee table and placed her hands on her hips. "You're not fooling me for one minute, Jane. You're not even excited to see you have a letter from Isaac, your supposed boyfriend."

"I don't get excited easily. I don't even know what it says yet."

"You're in love with my son, always have been."

Jane had no words for that comment. She reached forward and grabbed the letter. "I should read this."

"You read it. I'll put the coffee on, and then when I sit back down, we can talk." Sadie headed off to the kitchen.

Jane sat on the couch with her fingers trembling, half due to the cold and half from nerves about what the letter might say. Carefully, she ripped open the envelope.

Dear Jane,

This is a difficult letter to write. We've lived beside each other for so long and I knew I liked you, but it was only when you left to help out your friend that I knew the true extent of my feelings …

JANE READ ON. In the rest of the letter, he expressed his feelings toward her. Feelings that she didn't return. Maybe, just maybe if she hadn't seen Matt again, she might've fooled herself into thinking something could happen between them, a courting kind of relationship that would lead to marriage.

She folded the letter into three and set it onto her lap, and then she looked into the crackling fire as it sent off sheets of golden amber flames into the darkness of the chimney above. Isaac was a good man and he had that darling little girl who could keep her busy. A little girl who needed a mother so badly.

Maybe this was the right choice, the perfect choice.

Gott was giving her a lifeline so she could have children. Isaac was such a good man.

It would be silly to refuse him. Her own marriage to look forward to would certainly quell the pain she'd feel when Matt got married by his deadline of Christmas.

Sadie brought out a tray of coffee items and placed them on the low coffee table and then sat beside Jane. "Well?"

"He misses me."

"He tells you that, does he?"

"He does."

"Has he proposed to you yet?"

"Nee. Not in a letter."

"So he hasn't done so in that letter?"

Jane shook her head.

"Well, what is he waiting for?"

Jane decided it was time for the truth to come out. "I guess he's waiting on me to show some signs of liking him in return."

"That's simple, isn't it? Do that. Show some signs of liking him in return."

"You're right. Things sound so simple when they come out of your mouth, Sadie."

"Love shouldn't be so complicated. In my mind, if

love is complicated that means there's a problem. When he's the right one, you don't have to ask anyone their opinion because you know it in your heart." Sadie shook her head.

Jane looked at the large white coffeepot, knowing that Sadie was really talking about Matt. "Shall I pour?"

"Nee, I'll do it." Sadie poured out two coffees and then topped them with milk. "Two sugars for you isn't it?"

"Jah," Jane said feeling more like five spoonfuls of sugar to give her some much-needed energy.

"Don't look so worried all the time, Jane. You're making wrinkles on that pretty forehead of yours." She passed the coffee mug over to Jane.

"It's a little late for that, I'm afraid."

"Jane, it's not. You're always putting yourself down. I can hear it in the little things you say."

"Better to put myself down before other people do it."

"Nonsense. Let people say what they will."

Jane took a sip of coffee. "They probably wouldn't say it, but they'd think it. I'm too tall and I have red hair, which no one seems to like. They like dark hair or they like blonde, anything but red."

"Golden red hair is delightful, so unusual, so dreamy-like. And your skin is fair with sparkles here and there."

Jane smiled. "You've become a poet."

Sadie laughed. "I'm not trying to be. What's inside a person, that's what counts and you have that Jane. You have beauty on the inside *and* on the outside. What man could resist that combination?"

Jane sighed. She was doing a lot of that these days. "Only every man I've ever met so far."

"Rubbish."

"Well, I'm not married."

"Perhaps it's you who's your own worst enemy because you don't know your true worth. If you don't realize your true worth, how do you expect anybody else to?"

Jane's gaze dropped to the letter in her lap. "Perhaps Isaac realizes it." And for that reason maybe he deserved a chance. "I'll see what happens with him when I get back."

"Well don't take too long, will you? I don't approve of what Matt's doing."

"I won't."

"I just want you to both find happiness and love. I thought you'd do that together, but I guess it's not to be. Surely Matt must know which one he likes in his heart."

"I agree, Sadie. He's just waiting on my approval for the one he's chosen. I'm sure that's it."

"It wonders me he'd need anybody's approval if his love is love, truly love."

Jane sighed for the fifteenth time that day, feeling

sorry for herself. She was over thirty after all and had never even had one single marriage proposal. She was an oddity in her Amish community. "Perhaps I'll never be in love, not with anybody."

"You might be right, Jane. Not everybody finds love. It would be nice, but I know that not all find it."

Jane stared down into her coffee. The worst thing was that her love for Matt wasn't returned. It would've been far easier if she had never found anyone to love. That, she thought, she could've lived with.

CHAPTER 15

LANIE LOOKED out the window of her house and waited for the twins to arrive.

She had to take their measurements for their new dresses—something she'd promised them for going along with the ruse that she and Matt had created. She'd asked them to come promptly at three in the afternoon. That was naptime for her daughter. It was fortunate that at five years old Mary-Lee still had a one-hour nap in the afternoon.

At fifteen minutes after three, Lanie was starting to get upset. If they came when Mary-Lee was awake, she'd find it hard to concentrate, and concentration was something that was vital when it came to taking measurements.

The twins finally arrived at 3:25. Lanie stood at the

door and beckoned them over. When they got closer, she asked them to be quiet.

"Is Mary-Lee asleep now?" asked Anne.

"Jah."

"I was hoping to play with her."

Lanie gritted her teeth. "But remember, I asked you to come at three because that's what time she goes down for her nap."

"Isn't she too old for a nap?" Beatrice asked.

"Don't tell her that," Lanie said. "You don't want me to make any mistakes with these dresses, do you?"

"Nee."

"That's why I specifically asked you to get here at three on the dot."

"We're sorry. It's her fault," Anne said, nodding to Beatrice.

"I was finishing off a chore for *Mamm* and she wouldn't allow me to leave until it was done."

"Anyway, come in and please don't speak loudly."

While she took their measurements, she questioned them. She wasn't making them dresses for nothing. She needed information. "How was dinner with Jane and Sadie?"

"It was okay, but I don't know if we convinced Jane enough."

"Of course we did. She was totally convinced we're in love with Matt. And if he was interested in me, I wouldn't say no and that's the truth."

"Well he's not interested in you, Anne!" Lanie snapped.

"I know, but if he were …"

"He's not, so there's no point talking about it. This is all just pretend, make-believe."

Beatrice placed her hands on her hips. "And we still don't know why, or what this is all about. Is Jane supposed to like Matt, or what?"

"You don't have to know anything. That's why I'm making you these dresses. Ask no questions and you'll not be tempted to reveal secrets."

"Lanie's right, Bea. That's why we're getting these dresses, silly. So keep quiet."

"I was only asking."

Lanie stood up, rolling up the tape measure. "Do you want a new dress each or what? Don't forget they'll probably be the nicest ones you've ever had." She looked up and down at the dresses they'd no doubt sewn themselves. "No offense to you or your *mudder* or anything, but I am good at what I do."

"*Jah,* we know you are, Lanie."

"We are sorry. My *schweschder* is sorry and everyone is sorry. We won't ask again."

"Good! See that you don't." She leaned down once more and took a waist-to-floor measurement of Anne, and then jotted it on her notes. A few minutes later she asked, "And what did you both think of Jane?"

"So beautiful, just like a fairy," Beatrice said.

Anne screwed up her nose. "A fairy? Have you actually ever seen a fairy?"

"Nee, but that's what one would look like. That's what they look like in my mind all beautiful and elegant. She's tall and willowy, and when she walks, she glides like a swan."

"Why didn't you say she's like a swan, then?"

Beatrice giggled. "You can call her that. I say she's like a fairy. A garden fairy."

Lanie wasn't even sure what a fairy was, but now she was sure she wouldn't be able to get the idea of a garden fairy out of her head. Did Matt think Jane was swan-like, or fairy-like too? As a woman, she found it hard to judge the beauty of another woman. Wait. What did it matter? He was already in love with Jane. There had to be something she could do about that … for the sake of Mary-Lee.

THE NEXT DAY, Matt's conscience was bothering him again. He felt so wretched for deceiving Jane he felt he had to confess the whole thing to the bishop. Then, the bishop would guide him what to do from there. In the bottom of his heart, he knew he'd be told he needed to tell Jane everything. It would be embarrassing, but at least his conscience would be clear.

When he knocked on the door of the bishop's

house, he was faced with the bishop's adult son, Jeremiah. He was in his mid-thirties.

"Hi, Jeremiah. Is Bishop David home?"

"Nee, he's been called out. He won't be long. Care to wait?"

"Sure."

Jeremiah led him to a small room with nothing but two couches and a coffee table in between them. Jeremiah picked up a book and started reading.

Matt thought it odd that Jeremiah wasn't talking to him, but it did give him time to think. He normally would've talked to Lanie, but she'd encouraged him with the plan. It was mostly her idea, but he couldn't mention that to Bishop David. He had to take full responsibility.

Sitting there as he was, he felt a real fool as he imagined what the bishop would think of his elaborate plot.

He knew exactly what the bishop would say. *Why not just ask her to marry you?*

Then he'd have to tell the bishop he was a coward. A coward when it came to love.

He was there to get the bishop's advice and whatever he told him to do, he'd have to follow it to the letter. Even if it filled him with embarrassment and shame.

Matt's attention turned to Jeremiah as he sat quietly reading. He was the oldest of the bishop's and

Debra's nine children and the only one who still lived at home.

Most likely feeling Matt's concentrated gaze, Jeremiah looked up. "Anything I can help you with?"

Matt smiled. Jeremiah wouldn't be able to help him at all. In fact, Jeremiah might be the last person who would have any idea about women. *"Nee denke,* that's alright I will wait for the bishop."

"I'll see if *Mamm* can make us a cup of coffee and get us a slice of cake, eh?"

"I don't want to put her to any trouble."

"It's no trouble. She loves feeding people."

"Okay, that would be nice."

"It will give us something to do while we wait."

He looked around the well-ordered and scrupulously clean room. Nothing was out of place. In fact, it was so bare that there was nothing to be out of place. Only one small clock sat on the mantelpiece and one needle-worked scripture plaque hung on the wall in a dark varnished, wooden frame.

"Mamm's bringin' out something."

"That's very kind of her."

"Now what's the problem? I see Jane is back. Are you having women problems?"

Jeremiah smirked at him.

"Not exactly."

"It's okay if you want to talk to my *vadder* since he is the bishop and all, but I might be able to help man-to-man, might be able to give you some advice. I have had experience."

"Now if I had a problem concerning a certain woman, and I'm not saying that it is, how would you be able to help me since you are a single man?"

He raised a finger in the air. "Ah, good point. I might be a single man, but that doesn't mean I haven't been in love and haven't had some chances of being married. I've had two ladies who really wanted to marry me over the years, and I turned them both down. I did."

"Why would you turn them down?"

"I didn't feel they were right for me."

Matt had to wonder if that were true. "And do you regret turning them down?"

"I don't regret anything. I'm still waiting for the right woman."

"I admire your faith."

"It's not faith, it's sense."

"There are many attractive and single women in the community, are you saying there's not one who appeals to you?"

"*Nee*," he answered after a long hesitation. "I don't find myself drawn to any of them."

The bishop's wife brought out the cake, and the coffee in a teapot. "Matthew, it's nice to see you again. The bishop won't be long."

"I can't stay too long, but if I miss him I'll catch up

with him at the next meeting. It's not something that's urgently important."

"Very good." She put the tray down and passed him his coffee cup and saucer and then she passed one to her son.

"*Denke, Mamm.*"

"*Denke,* Mrs. Brewer."

When Mrs. Brewer left, Jeremiah grinned. "So from our conversation so far. I'm pretty sure it's a love story. Hopefully, a love story that's gonna have a good ending."

"Maybe it's a loved and lost story."

"Nah. Or have you lost your love and that's what you're upset about?"

"I don't know. I'm so confused about everything." He took a sip of coffee. It was strong almost to the point of being bitter. It was just like his mother made. He had used to like strong coffee like that in his younger days but now he liked it a little milder.

Once he finished his coffee, and Jeremiah was asking more probing questions about Jane, he figured he'd talk to the bishop some other time. Maybe *Gott* was prompting him to work these problems out for himself.

Matt gave heed to the promptings, and made his excuses to leave. One thing he knew, he didn't want to end up a single man like Jeremiah.

CHAPTER 16

JANE AND SADIE had just sat down with Lanie for their dinner when a knock sounded on the door.

"Who could that be at this hour?" Sadie said as she got up.

Jane hoped it was Matt.

"I'm sure I heard a car," said Lanie.

"I wasn't taking much notice."

Lanie kept talking to Jane, but Jane had one ear on the door, listening to see who it was. She got the surprise of her life when she heard Isaac's voice.

"Hello, Ma'am. I'm Isaac Egan, a friend of Jane's."

"You're … you're not Isaac, are you?"

Jane frowned. It *was* Isaac. This was dreadful. If only she hadn't mentioned Isaac to Sadie and exaggerated their relationship.

Isaac said, "I live right next to Jane and I just

happened to be in the area and I knew she was staying here."

Jane knew he hadn't 'just happened to be in the area.' He never went anywhere. He was a goat farmer and as long as she'd known him, he had trusted no one to look after his goats.

"Come in. This is perfect timing. We've only just sat down for dinner. Would you care to join us?"

"Would I ever. I've been traveling all day on the Greyhound with little to eat."

"Well, we have plenty. Come in. We're having corned beef, with white onion sauce and baked vegetables."

"That sounds, and smells, mouth-watering."

Jane bounded to her feet. "Isaac. What a surprise."

"Jane, it's so good to see you. Can I steal you away for a quick moment for a word? I know you're in the middle of dinner."

"Steal her away," Sadie said. "And we're not in the middle. We've barely started."

Jane walked with Isaac into the living room. "What are you doing here?"

"I missed you. I had to see you."

Jane's mouth dropped open and she covered it with her hand.

"Is it so shocking?"

"Kind of."

"You told Mrs. Yoder about me?"

"I mentioned you."

He smiled. "You must feel something for me to have mentioned me."

"Let's eat and then we can talk later, *jah?*"

"Sure. Are you pleased I came?"

That put her right on the spot.

NO!

She wasn't pleased that he had come.

Right now, she didn't need any further complications when she was in the middle of losing the only man she'd ever loved.

Matt would see Isaac, and Jane would slip further from his mind as a possible *fraa*.

Matt would think she was taken.

"Of course I'm pleased. Wait, where's Rosalee?"

"With my *mudder*."

They walked back into the room with the others and by this time, Sadie had set Isaac a place.

"You sit right next to Jane," Sadie said.

"*Denke*, that's very kind."

"You got here just in time for dinner, Isaac."

"Oh, Isaac, this is Lanie."

"Pleased to meet you, Lanie." They exchanged smiles while Jane filled his plate with food, and then placed it in front of him.

"*Denke*, Jane. This looks amazing."

Sadie felt the need to tell him, "Lanie is a widow with a young *dochder*."

Isaac said, "I'm a widower and I have a young *dochder* too."

"Oh, how old?" asked Lanie.

"Rosalee is five-years-old."

"So's Mary-Lee."

"You have things in common," said Jane, seeing the writing on the wall. He was going to fall in love with Lanie.

Isaac ate a mouthful before he said to Jane, "Probably not too much in common." He looked back at Lanie, "You see, I'm a goat farmer."

"I love goats. My family raised goats for the milk. We made cheese and yoghurt too. It was so much fun playing with the goats. Your *dochder* must enjoy it too, Isaac."

Isaac drew his eyebrows together. "There's not much time for play. It's mostly work."

With a sparkle in her eye, Sadie said, "Ah, but if you had a *fraa* to help you on the farm, it would be … there would be time for games and fun."

"You're probably right. Rosalee was only a few months old when her mother took ill."

"I'm sorry, Isaac," said Lanie. "I know what it's like to lose someone you love so much."

He smiled at her and gave a little nod. "Do you work, Lanie?"

"*Nee,* not really. I help my *bruder* out on his farm. I guess that's work. In exchange, I get to live in the small *haus* on his property. I'm getting the better end of the arrangement by far."

Jane had heard that Lanie sewed for a living, and wondered why she hadn't mentioned that.

"I'm sure it makes him happy to be looking after you," Isaac said.

"It does, I suppose."

Jane noticed Isaac's face come alive when he spoke to Lanie. This wasn't good. This was her backup man and the last thing she wanted was for him to have an interest in another woman.

But there was nothing she could do about it, nothing at all. And who wouldn't be attracted to her with her creamy skin, haunting dark eyes and raven black hair?

And he hadn't even met Mary-Lee yet and she was as cute as a button. Jane knew in her heart the two little girls would get along so well. They would be like twins.

Maybe she was destined to be alone, and if she couldn't have Matt, she was better off that way. It wouldn't be fair to marry a man who was her heart's second choice.

Unless … unless *Gott* had someone else for her, Jane thought. Someone she could love and who would love her in return.

"Where are you staying, Isaac?" asked Jane.

"Our bishop arranged for me to stay with Bishop David."

"That's perfect," said Lanie. "He lives up the road from me. I can drive you there when we're finished with dinner."

"That would be great, but I thought I might have a word with Jane before I leave if that's okay."

"I can wait for you."

When they'd finished a dessert of peach pie with cream, Sadie wasted no time making a suggestion. "Isaac, why don't you and Jane go to the living room and I'll stay here and talk with Lanie."

Isaac smiled. "Thank you."

Isaac and Jane walked into the living room and Jane quickly sat. She knew he'd want to discuss the letter he'd written. "Sit here beside me."

He sat down. "I hope you don't mind me coming to see you. I wasn't quite sure what I was walking into."

"That's okay. It's always nice to see you."

"I guess you got my letter?"

"I did and I have to say I was surprised by it. I thought we were friends."

"I hope you don't think I'm too forward in the letter. I've never said anything to you like that in person, but I figured you might have known my feelings for you without me having to say anything." He pushed his dark hair behind his ear. "Then I realized I might be wrong and I had to find you and tell you in person. As soon as I sent the letter I knew it wasn't enough. You can't say these things with just written words. I needed to look into your eyes."

"Do you mean, you still feel that way?"

"Of course, I only wrote the letter last week. What possibly could have changed?"

"Meeting Lanie." Jane decided the straightforward approach was the best. She had to figure this love thing out fast. She'd sensed something between the two of them right away.

"Jane, I don't know that woman. Never met her before. Why would meeting a woman for five minutes change my feelings for you?"

"I don't know, but that's the funny thing. How do you know what love is when you feel affection for someone … is that love? If you want to live with someone and look after them … well, isn't that what a *bruder* does for a *schweschder,* and that's not the kind of love we're talking about, but it's still a kind of love." Not the one she was looking for, though. Did Isaac have a brotherly love for her?

He narrowed his eyes and Jane saw it as confusion.

She tried to explain herself better. "Love needs to be all consuming, doesn't it? You only see that person, you only think about that one person. It's not a choice, as such."

A smile replaced Isaac's confusion. "Will you marry me, Jane?"

Jane's mouth fell open with shock. Someone had proposed. No longer would she be a woman with no choices. She was now a woman someone wanted. It felt good.

He continued, "Return with me now; marry me as soon as possible."

She always wanted something like this to happen. She couldn't say yes, but she was too cowardly to say no. What if this was her only chance of becoming a mother? Surely that would make up for everything. But, would it be fair to Isaac? "Can I have time to think it through?"

"Of course. I know this has come as quite a shock to you. Take all the time you need. As long as you can give me a yes at the end."

They smiled at each other. She was grateful to be loved, to be given that chance for happiness. Isaac was a good man. She'd always respected him. "I can't believe you came all this way."

"I thought I should. Just in case you fell in love with someone here. I never would've forgiven myself. I didn't want to hold back any longer."

"That never would've happened. This is my old community. I know most of the people here."

"I know, you said that. You told me your father moved over here, then your mother joined him and then years later you moved back to Ohio."

"That's right and that's why I feel like I have two

homes. This is where I grew up, mostly."

Jane was grown up on the outside, but inside she felt just like a young girl. She did all the grown-up things, had a job, paid the bills, but just like any little girl who sometimes needed a good mother and her father, she also needed. What made her feel more alone was that her sister and brother had left the community and she'd not heard from them since.

"I should go. I think Lanie wants to go, and the bishop will most likely want to talk with me when I get back. It'd be rude to get back there too late."

"That's fine. I agree."

"What are you doing tomorrow?"

"Oh, Isaac, I'm sorry, but I don't really have any free time while I'm here. I came here to help out a friend. It's been quite time consuming so far." She had to keep the two men apart, but how could she now that Sadie knew about Isaac?

"Could you squeeze in lunch with me tomorrow?"

She owed him that much for coming so far to see her. "Yes, I think I could do that. We could have a quick lunch somewhere. But neither of us have use of a horse and buggy. Unless, you do?"

"I'm sure I can borrow one from Bishop David."

"That sounds good, and how long will you be here for?"

"Just a few days and then I have to get back. It was

tough getting someone to mind the place. That's why…"

"I know, that's why you can never go on a vacation."

"That's right. But if we get married, if you accept my proposal, I will do my best to try to get away every few years and go somewhere nice. I have relatives all over the country we can stay with."

"Sounds wonderful."

"Is that a yes?" he joked.

She giggled. "No. It's not."

"I'll collect you at eleven."

"Perfect."

CHAPTER 17

FIFTEEN MINUTES LATER, Sadie and Jane watched Lanie and Isaac leave. Once the horse and buggy were out of sight, Sadie closed the door. "What did he say to you?"

"I shouldn't be telling you."

"I'm your friend, aren't I?"

"That's true, and I do need someone to talk to. He asked me to marry him."

Sadie's mouth turned up at the corners, causing her cheeks to look even fuller. She pulled Jane over to the couch. "I thought so. Why else would he have come out all this way?"

"Maybe *Gott* brought him here to meet Lanie."

"Jane, take a good look at yourself without your negativity. He was politely talking to that woman. He has no interest in her, and she's too young for him."

"But isn't being young a good advantage? Don't men prefer younger women? Matt doesn't seem to mind. Look at Abigail."

"Nee, Jane. They prefer someone they can talk with, someone who can be a friend, and a companion."

"He did say he wasn't interested in Lanie."

Sadie gasped. "Oh, Jane, you didn't ask him, did you?"

"I did. I thought it would be okay."

"Why ever would you ask such a thing?"

"I had to know the truth. It seemed they were getting along great and their *kinner* would too. They could have a perfect family if they married. He's lost a *fraa* and she's lost a husband. Each would know the other's sadness and pain."

"You shouldn't have opened your mouth about things like that. He probably wouldn't have considered her before now, and now he could think that she's a possibility."

Jane giggled. "Who's being negative now?"

Sadie smiled. "That's true. You're rubbing off on me. It should be the other way around. Whatever is good, just and pure, we should think on those things."

"I know. It's true. Let's clear away the dishes and then I'll make you a nice cup of coffee."

"Denke, Jane, that sounds lovely."

LANIE LOOKED over at the man beside her and wondered if he'd been sent to her from *Gott*. Matt only had eyes for Jane, so was this man meant for her? Only thing was, she was certain that he too was in love with Jane. She had to do her best to change his mind.

"My *dochder* is staying with my *mudder* tonight. I'm blessed I have her to help me out when I need it. I normally take her everywhere with me, but I had gotten a feeling that Jane might not be too fond of children."

"That's wrong. Jane loves children. She's so good with Rosalee."

"What a delightful name."

"Thank you."

"Jane might only like certain children, the ones she knows well then."

"It's possible, I suppose, but don't we all like our own better than anyone else's?"

She giggled. "I guess that's true. If poor old Jane ever has her own, she'll be a changed woman. She'd have to love her own *kinner*."

"When did your husband die, if I might ask?"

"Just over a year ago."

"I'm sorry to hear that."

"And your *fraa?*"

"She died when Rosalee was only two months old."

"Oh, that's seriously tragic."

"It was influenza. A particular bad strain, they told

me. Two others in our community died from it that year."

"My husband had a heart condition. They didn't know how long he had. He was here one day and gone the next. Even though I knew it could happen, it still came as a shock."

"It's good you have your family close by."

"And you?"

"My family disowned me when I joined the Amish at nineteen."

"Oh, how romantic. You joined for your *fraa?*"

"*Nee.* I didn't know her then. I met her a few months after I'd officially joined, and got to know her over the next couple of years and then we got married."

"So, you just up and joined … why?"

"Because I knew there was a better way, a better lifestyle. I wanted to put away distraction, work with my hands and concentrate on living a Godly life."

Lanie was impressed. He was such a good man with good principles. It annoyed her that two men she liked were both in love with Jane. Which one would Jane choose? She guessed that was why Isaac had followed Jane all the way from Ohio. "Do you have any plans while you're here?"

"Only to have lunch with Jane tomorrow. Apart from that, we've not planned anything else."

"It sounds *wunderbaar.*" She steered the horse into the bishop's driveway and drove the horse and buggy all the way to the house. "I hope you have a nice stay while you're here, Isaac."

He got out of the buggy. "Thank you, Lanie, and thanks for the ride."

They exchanged smiles.

Lanie made her way back down the driveway. What she had to do was clear. She had to stick to Jane like glue. And, she had to get to know Isaac a whole lot better before he left.

CHAPTER 18

THE NEXT MORNING, Matt came to collect Jane, and Sadie was right there to keep Matt up to date with recent goings on.

"Jane had a visitor last night," Sadie was quick to tell him.

"Oh? Who was it?" Matt asked, sinking into the couch.

"Someone from her community ... and he came with a proposal."

Jane heard what was being said from the kitchen. She put the last dish away, and folded the tea towel over the tap to dry.

"For Jane?" Matt asked.

"Of course for Jane."

Jane walked into the living room. "Sadie! I told you that in the strictest confidence."

"Proposal for what?" Matt asked looking blankly between the two of them.

"Proposal for marriage, of course, what else would he propose about?" asked Sadie.

Matt tilted his head to one side. "Someone has proposed marriage to you, Jane?"

"That's right."

"I thought you'd never marry."

"Well, you were wrong. I will." She noticed he gulped.

"So you said yes?" His eyes opened wide.

"She's considering it," Sadie answered for her.

"Sadie, please." Jane then looked at Matt, and sat down beside him. "Please don't let anyone know about this. Isaac wouldn't want anybody to know."

"Especially if she refuses him," said Sadie.

Matt shrugged. "Who is this 'Isaac' person?"

"He's a neighbor of mine."

"*Jah,* and he chased her all the way over here just to make sure she wouldn't forget him. He wants to marry her."

"You said that once or twice now, *Mamm.*" He looked from his mother to Jane.

"You never mentioned anyone called Isaac in any of the letters."

"Well, I didn't tell you about everything just like you didn't tell me everything about your intentions with these five women."

"I see."

Isaac did make her feel special. He had followed her and stated his intentions. That was something she wished Matt had done.

Jane hoped that Matt was jealous, but she didn't even consider that possible. She'd seen the competition and all of them were far more pleasing to the eye than she was.

"Oh, did you have big plans for us today?" Jane asked. "I'm hoping that whatever it is won't take too long."

"Why?"

"I told Isaac I'd go to lunch with him."

Matt's shoulder's drooped. "You're here to see me. Not to go to lunch with someone you can see when you're at home."

"*Ach*, Matt, stop being such a *boppli*," Sadie crowed.

Jane found that a little bit funny and couldn't keep the smile from her face. "It'll just be a quick lunch for the very reason you mentioned. I told him I was here helping you with something."

"Did he ask what?"

"I don't recall that he did. Anyway, I didn't—and I won't—tell him."

"What time is he calling for you?"

"About eleven, he said."

"Then you're mine for two hours?"

"I guess."

"Come on let's go." Once they were in the buggy and turning onto the road, Matt said, "Tell me about Isaac."

"Like I said, he's my neighbor. A widower with a young girl."

"You forgot the part about him being in love with you."

Jane looked at the fields they were passing.

Matt continued, "I'm your friend. Haven't I told you all the details about my life? Don't you think I should have that in return?"

"To tell you the complete and honest truth, Matt, I really don't think I know you anymore."

He took his eyes off the road and stared at her.

"Why would you say that?"

She breathed out heavily. "All this about you not knowing who you want to marry. It's all a bit strange. Do you want to choose between these women as if one woman is practically the same as another? It seems a cold approach and I never saw you as a cold person."

"I'm sorry you feel that way, but that's not the way I see it. I've come to a certain age and I do want marriage and everything that goes along with it. I want a family to look after, Jane, don't you understand that?"

"I'm sorry, I shouldn't have said how I really feel. I wouldn't have if I had known you'd get upset."

"I'm not upset. I'm pleased that you … um, respect me enough to tell me your true opinion."

"When does love come into it with you? Don't you think it's important to love someone before you are married?" Jane asked.

"That's the way I've always hoped it would be … love, marriage, *bopplis*."

She smiled when he smiled at her.

"Don't you want that, Jane?"

"That's what I've always wanted."

She saw him swallow hard. "Jane, have you ever been in love?"

"*Jah*, I have been."

"And who is he, or who was he?"

Her heart froze. She didn't know what to say. When she opened her mouth, desperately hoping the perfect words would somehow spill out, she looked up the road and saw a buggy heading toward them.

He saw it too and squinted. "That looks like Lanie. I wonder what she's doing out this way."

Jane was saved from answering the question. *What a relief!* She hoped he wouldn't ask it again. If he asked straight out, it would be hard to tell him a lie. But she might have to tell a quick lie to save everybody from embarrassment.

When the buggies came level to each other, Matt pulled his horse up and Lanie also stopped. "Where are you off to?" he asked.

"Back to your *mudder's haus*. I think I left my coat there last night."

Jane remember that Lanie had been wearing her coat last night. What was she playing at? "I think I saw you leaving in your coat."

"Really?"

Jane nodded.

"That is strange. I can't find it anywhere at home."

"Maybe I'm wrong," Jane said, with a quick shrug.

"It won't hurt to ask her. *Mamm's* home."

"What are you two doing today?" Lanie asked.

"Nothing in particular. I just thought I needed to take Jane out give her a break from being home with my *mudder* all day."

"I'll keep Sadie entertained for a while, then." Lanie offered him a big smile.

Jane knew that Lanie was trying to get on Matt's good side and his mother's. If Sadie really liked Lanie it would make things easier for Matt. It was an obvious ploy, but probably a good one.

They said their goodbyes when a car appeared behind Lanie, and then the horses and buggies continued on their separate ways.

"What do you think of Lanie?" asked Matt.

"I like her. She's intelligent and mature and ready to settle down. She already has Mary-Lee and I'm sure she doesn't want her to be an only child."

"For sure."

Jane waited for him to say more but that's all he said about her.

"Are you going to marry Isaac?" he asked.

"Do you really want to talk about this? I'm here now because of you and who you're going to marry not the other way around."

He chuckled. "That's how it started out, I'm not so sure it's going to end that way."

"What do you mean?"

"We could have all kinds of men coming to look for you, asking for your hand in marriage."

"That is very unlikely."

"I don't think so. You could have five, and maybe I'll be helping you to choose between them."

"Nee, that would never happen. I can make up my own mind. We are here to find you a *fraa.* That's all I want to think about."

"So you haven't given an answer?"

Was he talking about Isaac? *"About what?"*

"An answer about marriage to Isaac."

"Nee, I haven't given him an answer. And I'd rather not talk about myself or my life. I'll find you a *fraa,* I'll go home and then we may or may not keep writing to one another. Those letters will have to include your wife of course, once you're a married man."

"And your new husband," he shot straight back at her.

She glanced over at him disapprovingly, and shook her head.

CHAPTER 19

LANIE STOOD on Sadie's front porch and knocked on her door.

Sadie opened it, and Lanie was pleased to see a smile on her face. "Lanie, it's nice to see you again."

"*Denke*. Did I leave a coat here last night?"

"I don't think so. Come in and we'll take a look around."

Lanie stepped through the door.

Sadie looked on the pegs behind the door. "It's not here. I'll take a look in the kitchen."

Lanie followed her in, pulled out a chair and sat down.

"It's not here either."

Lanie threw up her hands. "I've got no idea what I've done with it."

Sadie looked at her. "Aren't you wearing it?"

Lanie looked down at the black coat she was wearing. She'd been caught out. How stupid was she? "Oh! This is a spare."

"Care for a cup of hot tea?"

"I'd love one. If you have the time to spare."

"I do. Where is little Mary-Lee?"

"With my *mudder*. She wanted to keep her for another day. And, Mary-Lee just loves her *grossmammi.*" Lanie said. Sadie was possibly going to be her mother-in-law, so she wanted to start impressing her right away. "I'll make it for us." Once in the kitchen, Lanie pulled out a chair for Sadie to sit in. Then Lanie filled up the teakettle and popped it on the stove, talking as she moved. "What do you think of Isaac just coming here like that? No one was expecting him, were they?"

"Nee. He came here for Jane."

"I thought so. He's in love with her. He came here to take her back with him it seems." She turned on the gas and then sat down in front of Sadie.

"You might as well know as long as you don't say anything. He's proposed to her."

That ruled Isaac out ... maybe. Or, maybe she had to concentrate on Isaac before he left. "Is that right?"

"It certainly is. He seems a very nice man."

"He does, but how will he cope with seeing Jane with Matt? I just saw them passing me in the buggy just now."

"They're just friends, they keep telling everyone that."

"What does Jane think? Has she answered Isaac—accepted his proposal? Are they getting married?"

"All I know is that Jane was shocked to see him."

Lanie leaned closer, "Has she said yes?"

"Nee. She hasn't said yes but they're going to have lunch together today. He will try to talk her into it for sure. "

"I've never seen Jane as the marrying kind," Lanie said.

"Funny you say that because neither does my son."

"You've talked about Jane with Matt?"

"I have," Sadie answered. "So you want to marry my son?"

Lanie hadn't been prepared for that question—hadn't expected Sadie to be so open about this project. "I do like him and have made no secret of it."

"Oh, so does Matt know?"

"I haven't specifically told him."

"Who have you told?"

Lanie giggled. "No one. I don't intend to make a secret of it. Perhaps that's what I should've said."

"Are you prepared to marry again, so soon?"

"I think it will help take away the pain. He won't be a replacement for Desmond. The two of them are very different. Desmond was a very gentle man and Matt is more forthright. I think he'll make a wonderful *vadder* and wonderful husband."

"Oh, there's no doubt about that. There are four other women who think the same, as you probably already know."

"I found that out. The twins, and Marcy, and her cousin, Abigail."

"It's not nice."

"I know, but what am I to do?"

"I've been thinking of something and it's kept me up all night. Both Jane and I thought you got along well with Isaac. Why don't you marry him and leave Matt for Jane?"

Lanie was horrified. Sadie didn't like her; didn't want her for a daughter-in-law. What's more, she wanted Jane to marry Matt. This was dreadful.

Leave Matt for Jane, echoed inside Lanie's head.

"Sadie, are you saying that you don't think I'm a good match with your son?" She desperately wanted Sadie to take the words back.

"I've always thought that Jane and Matt would marry, and I'm having trouble ever seeing him with anybody else. It's nothing personal, Lanie. I am very fond of you."

Lanie was pleased to hear it. Apparently she just wasn't as fond of her as she was of Jane.

At that moment, the kettle whistled.

"I think I have some chocolate chip cookies in that

blue cookie jar on the top of the counter."

"Perfect, I'll fetch us some." While Lanie found the cookies and placed some onto a plate, Sadie got up and made the tea.

"Let's take this and have it in front of the fire," Sadie said once the tea was steeping.

"*Jah*, that sounds lovely."

They sat down on the couch, and had a silent moment. Then Sadie poured them each a cup of tea.

"Sadie, I have to ask you something."

Sadie looked at her, and then sat her teacup in the saucer. "Go ahead."

"Do you think that Jane is in love with Matt?"

Sadie sighed. "That's what I always hoped and then Isaac showed up. I did ask her and she told me she had someone back home."

"So she mentioned Isaac to you when she first arrived?"

"Not right away, but his name did come up."

Lanie wanted to be sure. "When you say his name came up, did she say she was in love with Isaac?"

"Not in so many words." Sadie sipped on her tea. "Why? Are you afraid she'll take Matt from you?"

Lanie giggled. Sadie could see straight through her. "*Ach nee*. I was just … I just want Matt to end up being with someone who truly loves him."

"How can he fail when there are five women who say they truly love him?"

Lanie fixed a smile on her face. Sadie's words reminded her to stick to the plan Matt and she had devised. Jane could marry Isaac, and she'd have Matt. "That's true."

"He's very blessed."

"He truly is. It's true."

Sadie kicked off her shoes and continued, "If you ask me, I don't see him with one of the twins. He's more suited to someone older, someone more mature like either you or Marcy."

Lanie was glad to hear it. *"Denke."*

"I only hope that he sees that."

"I'm sure he will. He was probably only considering them because they like him, and they let him know it."

"That wouldn't have happened in my day," Sadie said. "These days women are far too forward."

"Jah, I know what you mean." Lanie drank her tea as fast as she could. It was awkward sitting there with Sadie when the woman didn't approve of what was going on. She saw that Sadie was drinking her tea just as quickly. When they both had finished, Lanie sat her teacup on the saucer and set both down on the coffee table. "I should go."

"Okay. *Denke* for stopping by. If I find your coat, I'll have Matt drop it by."

"That would be good, *denke."* Lanie leaned forward and took both cups and saucers. "I'll rinse these before I go."

"Leave them. There's no need."

"It's fine." Lanie took the dishes to the kitchen and washed them out, dried them and left them on the counter. She then went back out and said goodbye to Sadie.

When she was in her horse and buggy, a little way down the road, she saw the bishop's tall bay horse coming toward her. In her heart, she knew it was Isaac driving the buggy. She slowed her horse and then she stopped the buggy on the quiet country road. He pulled up beside her.

As soon as she saw his handsome face, she forgot all about her thought of minutes ago—the one where she didn't mind if Isaac and Jane married.

"Hello, Lanie. We meet again."

"Hi, Isaac. Are you heading to see Jane?"

"I am. Where are you headed?"

She didn't tell him Jane wasn't back yet. "I couldn't find my coat and I thought I might've left it at Sadie's *haus*. It wasn't there."

He smiled and looked in the buggy. "Where's your *dochder?*"

"*Ach*, I couldn't get her back from my *mudder*. She wanted to keep her an extra day and Mary-Lee wanted to stay too. It'll give me more time to get some work done."

"What kind of work do you do?"

"I'm a seamstress. I work from home. I make

dresses, suits, and I also do mending repairs for some of the local tailors and dry cleaners. I like to keep busy." She then remembered she'd told him something entirely different the day before. Now she had let him know she was fully self-sufficient. She knew men liked to look after women.

"That's good. It's good to do that."

"I might see you soon, then." She smiled, relieved he hadn't noticed her gaffe. When she saw he wasn't going to say anything else, she didn't want to stay too long, and quickly moved her horse forward. "I might see you around, Isaac."

"Bye, Lanie," he called after her.

Lanie had to get home to make dresses. She'd promised the twins a new dress each for going along with her and Matt's elaborate plan. Abigail and Marcy were a different story. They genuinely liked him. Still, they all knew it was a set-up and those two also knew Matt wasn't interested in either of them. She couldn't blame them for holding out hope.

From Lanie's end, the only way she could get Matt to commit to her was for him to finally put Jane behind him. He never outright said as much, but she knew Matt was pining for Jane. She only hoped Jane didn't feel the same. If Jane loved Matt then surely she would never have moved to Ohio.

The troubling question was, why had Jane never married?

CHAPTER 20

Isaac got out of his buggy and secured the horse to the hitching post. As he approached the house, the front door opened and he plastered a grin over his face, expecting to see Jane. Instead, a large woman filled the doorway. It was Sadie.

"*Wie ghets,* Mrs. Yoder."

"Just call me Sadie," she said with a laugh. "I'm popular today, but I'm sure you're not here to see me."

"I did arrange to meet Jane here at eleven."

"You're a bit early. It's only half past ten."

"Is she not here?"

"*Nee,* she's gone out with my son, Matt. They should be back any time though. She hadn't forgotten about you picking her up at eleven. The kettle is boiled if you'd like to sit and wait with a cup of coffee or tea?"

"I'd love a cup of coffee if you're having one."

"I'll be glad to have one. And I might be able to find some chocolate chip cookies." She opened the door wider and he walked through.

"Have you had another visitor this morning? You said you were 'popular today.'"

"Jah, that's right. Lanie was here."

"Oh, that's right she said she'd left her coat here. I met her on the roadway."

"We had a nice conversation over a cup of tea."

"That's good."

"You sit in front of the fire, now, and I'll get you that coffee."

As soon as Isaac sat on the couch, a Mr. Grover jumped onto the couch next to him giving him a fright. The cat then stared at Isaac, who slowly put out his hand toward him. Mr. Grover sniffed his hand and then moved toward him and tucked his head under Isaac's hand, responding with loud purring.

"I don't like cats," Isaac said under his breath.

"That's Mr. Grover," Sadie said as she brought out a large tray that contained only two small cups of coffee and a couple of cookies on a plate.

"Well, hello, Mr. Grover."

The cat proceeded to sit on his lap.

"Get off," Sadie said pushing the cat away. "There. Now you can drink your coffee," she said to Isaac.

Isaac leaned forward and took one of the small cups

while Sadie sat next to him. After he took a sip, he said, "This is very strong coffee."

"That's why I serve it in the small cups. Oh, do you take milk or sugar? Maybe cream? I forgot to ask."

He shook his head. "Just black's fine for me, thanks. That's how I have it, too."

When Sadie got herself comfortable, Mr. Grover jumped back onto the couch and stared at Isaac.

"He likes you. He normally doesn't take to strangers."

"All animals like me."

"Do you have any pets?"

"I have a goat farm and they are my pets too. It's hard for people to understand, but it's true. They each have their own personality."

"Ah, that's right you said last night that you had the goat farm."

"No pets beyond the dog that helps me on the farm. He's not much of a pet, he's too old for that now. I'm sure my *dochder* would like a pet when she gets old enough to ask. I might allow her to have some when she's old enough to look after them. I don't have the time."

"That's a good idea, and by that time, she should be able to look after them herself, as you said. It teaches them responsibility."

"That's the idea," he said with a smile.

"Tell me about you and Jane."

He nearly choked on his coffee, and then he looked over at her.

"We've always gotten along. We didn't really have much to do with each other though, before my wife died. She'd only moved in next door a few months before Rosalee was born. Then, soon afterward, is when my wife died and everything changed for me. I had to just keep going with the farm, and the ladies helped me with Rosalee. That's when I really met Jane, and then slowly we got to know each other.

When Jane up and left suddenly, I knew I didn't want to be without her. I saw that as a real possibility, and that's why I wasted no time getting myself here."

It had been an awkward question and he really hadn't wanted to answer it, but neither did he want to be rude to the person Jane was staying with. Jane was still deciding how to answer his proposal, and if he got this woman offside, Jane could very well see that as a sign to say no to him.

"I'm sure Jane appreciates your honesty. And you made a big effort to be here, leaving your farm and your *dochder*."

"*Denke*, Sadie. I hope she sees it that way."

"I'm sure she does."

When they heard the sounds of a horse and buggy, Sadie got up and looked out the window. "Here they are, back with ten minutes to spare before eleven."

"Perfect timing," Isaac said.

MATT SAW THE BUGGY, one that he recognized as the bishop's, parked outside his mother's house. He said to Jane. "It seems your admirer is keenly waiting for you."

"Maybe."

"I'll come in with you and find out."

That was a dreadful idea. Jane had to keep them apart. "There's no need to for you to do that."

"That's fine. I'm *keen* to meet him since he's a friend of yours."

There was nothing Jane could do to keep them apart. Matt walked with Jane into the house. Sadie opened the door for them and then introduced Matt to Isaac.

The air was thick with tension as the two men sized each other up.

"What brings you here, Isaac?" Matt asked getting to the point.

"Jane does," was all that he said.

Matt raised his eyebrows. He wasn't expecting such an abrupt answer. In Matt's mind, Jane was his. This didn't sit well. The worst thing was, Jane had no idea how he felt. But if she did, would she even consider him?

"Goodbye, Jane." Matt smiled at Jane and then looked at his mother. After he gave her a nod, he said,

"Mamm."

"Are you coming back for dinner tonight?" Sadie asked.

"Jah, Mamm, I'll be back for dinner." He gave Isaac a nod as well, and then walked out the door closing it gently behind him. As he walked to the buggy, he hoped that him accepting the dinner invitation would stop Isaac from having dinner there as well.

And it did.

CHAPTER 21

JANE DIDN'T KNOW what to say to Isaac. She knew how to deal with him as a friend but now that he'd confessed his love for her, she didn't know how to react. She probably would've married him if she'd never met Matt, but she *had* met him. Had grown up with him, still loved him.

The question she had to consider was, once Matt married someone else, should she then marry for the sake of having a family and *kinner?* She was now alone in life with no family. For so many years she'd longed to belong somewhere, with someone.

Every Christmas, and every other sort of celebration, she had to rely on invitations from friends. She'd much rather have the celebration at her own home with her very own family.

In her heart, she knew there was still a chance of

motherhood. Maybe God sent her Isaac to show her that all was not lost.

"How about this table?" Isaac said pulling out a chair for her to sit in.

"Yes, looks perfect." She sat down, pulled her thoughts together, and took a deep breath hoping that he would say something so she wouldn't have to lead the conversation.

"I hope you don't mind me arriving here suddenly like I did." He studied her face.

"Not at all, but it was a surprise to see you."

He took one of the menus that was wedged between the salt and pepper shakers, handed it her and then took one for himself. "I'm ravenous."

"Don't they feed you where you're staying?"

He laughed. "They do, but I wasn't very hungry this morning and I pretty much skipped breakfast. I plan on making up for it now."

"Please do."

When they each had a burger and fries in front of them, he took a mouthful then wiped his hands on a napkin. "That is so good," he raved, after he'd chewed and swallowed.

"Yes, they do make a nice hamburger. I've been here before once or twice."

"After you left to come here, I got to thinking about something you had said."

She'd just taken a mouthful and could only raise her eyebrows to signal that he should continue.

"You said your friend, Matt, wanted to speak to you urgently. I've heard you speak of Matt—speak of him very affectionately. And I happen to know he's not a married man. I asked around, and besides that you've never mentioned he had a wife, and then I got to thinking it could only be one thing."

She swallowed a mouthful. "And what's that?"

"I'm guessing he's going to ask you to marry him. Am I right? That is, if he hasn't already."

If only it were true. It was too embarrassing to tell him why she was there. And the fact that Matt had overlooked her completely was equally embarrassing. "At the moment, the reason I'm here is to help him with something that is confidential. It's nothing really. It's nothing to make a fuss of, and it's not what you just said."

"It's not?" He searched her face.

"No, it's not. It's not that at all."

"I'm glad to hear it. I'm delighted to hear that. I wasn't certain what the relationship you had with him was. I knew you were friends, good friends."

"Yes, good friends and that's the end of it."

"Will you consider my question?"

"I will—I already have been. It has come as a bit of a shock and I just need time to get used to the idea."

He smiled. "Rosalee loves you and we would have a perfect life together."

He was probably right, but she didn't know if she could overlook the fact that her heart burned for someone else. Would that be fair to Isaac? Even though her stomach was churning, she ate as much as she could of her hamburger, and could only manage a few of the French fries.

As Isaac was driving her back to Sadie's *haus*, he said, "Jane, I've come a long way to see you. Couldn't you spare me one full day?"

Jane was a little annoyed. She had never asked him to come there, and he worded it as though she owed him something. "I am here to help Matt with something, though. I explained that."

"Just one day?"

Jane figured it was better to get that one-day over with quickly. If Matt had plans she could have him change them. She knew she'd see him for dinner that night. "Okay, tomorrow, but then I really must be available to help Matt."

"Thank you, and then will you tell me what you're helping him with?"

"I can't."

"It's a secret?"

"Not really. Well, maybe it is. All I know is I can't tell you right now."

Isaac smiled. "I'll look forward to tomorrow. I'll plan something nice."

Jane stopped peeling the potatoes and stared at Sadie, wondering what it could be. "What's that?"

Sadie, seated opposite, kept shelling peas. "I heard you talking to yourself the other night. I know you're in love with my son. This day, there is no use denying it."

This was dreadful, and what did she mean by saying 'this day' there was no use denying it? She remembered Sadie's mother came from the Swiss Amish rather than being of German origins, so it might've been something they'd say. "You didn't tell him, did you?"

"I didn't. But if you feel that way about him, you must say something."

"Why, to embarrass myself completely? I've been rejected by him so many times that I can't take one more rejection."

"When did he ever reject you?"

"He didn't, not with words. But he ignored me for so many years. The elders forced us apart, and then when we were older he never came back to me. Then he courted a couple of girls. I'll never forget that."

"He took a few girls on buggy rides. It was nothing.

He never had a real girlfriend, someone he was seriously courting. I would've known about it."

Jane remained silent, as she dug the tip of the knife into one of the potatoes to remove an eye. Many Amish couples courted in secret and only told their parents when they were ready to marry. It was quite possible that Matt had courted many women. Who would know? "I guess that might be true because he didn't marry from amongst them."

"That's right, because they weren't you."

Jane smiled, appreciating Sadie's efforts. If only Matt believed they belonged together as strongly as his mother did. "I left when I was twenty-five and he did nothing about it. All he did was write to me just like someone would write to a friend, or a pen pal. If I'd meant anything to him, he would've come to fetch me and asked me to marry him."

"Men are stupid sometimes."

"If he loved me, he'd say so. If he loved me, he certainly wouldn't have brought me back to help him choose a wife. That's rubbing it in my face."

"Maybe, but consider that maybe it's easier now for him to see who the real one is that he loves."

"He hasn't come to that realization so far."

"How do you know it?"

Jane stared at Sadie. "Has he said anything to you about me?"

"Nee." Sadie shook her head.

The last spark of Jane's hope faded away. "It's no use. There's no point. I can't force somebody to love me."

"You're the perfect woman for him, Jane. You're so similar, so well suited to one another. I thought deep down that you always loved him. It just made sense. The two of you just make sense."

Jane laughed. If she didn't laugh, she'd cry. "It feels much better to hear you say that. At least we can both see it even if Matt can't. It doesn't matter what we think, though."

Sadie rubbed Jane's arm. "Do you want me to say something to him?"

"Oh no, that would be dreadful. Please don't say anything."

"I won't. I'll keep your secret, but I do think you should. The time to say something to him is now."

"What's the point of that? He already has five to choose from and I don't think he needs six. Anyway, I won't be counted among them. If he can't make up his mind, I can't help him."

"Maybe he has no idea that you're even interested in him."

Jane considered what Sadie had said.

Sadie continued, "Just give it some prayer, and some thought. Just make sure that you do something."

"*Jah,* I will think about it. Now, can we talk about something else?"

Over a dinner of ham, and baked vegetables that night, Matt looked bothered to learn that Jane had agreed to spend the whole of the next day with Isaac.

"I'm sorry, Matt, but he's come all this way. I'll stay an extra day to make up for it."

"*Denke,* Jane. I appreciate it, but you can see him every day when you're at home."

"I know that. It's just one day."

Matt nodded. "What does he want you to do?"

"I don't know what he's got in mind."

Matt didn't want to sound too bothered about it. But he knew he'd have to step things up or risk losing her.

CHAPTER 22

"I'M SO PLEASED to be spending the day with you, Jane."

Jane wasn't so certain her feelings agreed. "Yes, it will be good. I haven't seen you since … yesterday."

He threw his head back and laughed. "Even though we live next door to one another, we don't really spend much time together."

"That's true."

"But before we go anywhere …"

Jane looked over at him wondering what he was going to say.

"I feel you should talk to the bishop's wife."

"Debra?"

"Yes, Debra."

"Why do you think I should talk with her?"

"Because I don't think you've really talked to her since you've been here, have you?"

Jane thought back. "I'm not sure. Is someone complaining that I haven't spoken to her? I saw her at the meeting only on Sunday."

"But did you talk with her?"

"Yes, a little."

"You might not know this, Jane, because you didn't visit many communities, but you should really speak to the bishops and their wives at all the different places, more than just saying hello."

She stared at Isaac. "It's a little different because I know them so well. I grew up here, remember? You hardly go anywhere, so where is this coming from?"

"Before I married and had the goat farm, I traveled around to different communities—that's how I met my *fraa*."

"Sure, I'll go speak to Debra. But I'm sure she'll be busy with something more important."

"And what could be more important than you?"

"I can think of a good many things that would be more important than me."

He laughed at her, but Jane knew this was going to be awkward, and a huge waste of everyone's time. She had no idea why he was forcing her to do this.

And then Jane wondered whether the bishop's wife had something she wanted to say to her. Had she behaved inappropriately at the meeting or had she done or said something that she shouldn't? She couldn't think of anything like that.

"Do you know if she's home?" Jane asked.

"She was when I left. I didn't tell her that I was coming back with you. Such a worrier you are, Jane."

"I never thought of myself as a worrier, but you're not the first person to say that."

When they reached the bishop's house, Isaac stayed with the horse and put the reins over the hitching post while Jane knocked on the door.

Debra opened the door and smiled when she saw Jane's face. "Jane, how lovely to see you."

"*Denke.* I was about to spend some time with your *haus* guest, Matt… ooh, I mean… "

"Do you mean Isaac?"

"*Jah,* I was spending the day with Isaac and I realized I didn't say much to you on Sunday and I just came to have a little talk, if that's alright."

"Certainly Jane, you can talk to me about anything you like. Will Isaac be joining us for this talk?"

"It's not really a talk I just called in to say hello … more or less."

"Yes, that's quite alright. I thought you had something to talk to me about, maybe a confession."

Jane giggled. "*Nee,* I don't have any confessions to make about anything. Maybe I do, but I can't remember what they are right now."

Debra smiled. "Don't worry we all have our secrets

and that's okay. Come through into the kitchen and I'll make tea for three." Debra laughed. "That rhymes, tea for three."

"Jah, it does."

When they got to the kitchen, Debra directed her to sit on one of the four chairs at the small round table. "He likes my cooking too much."

Jane looked up at her. "Who does?"

"Jeremiah."

Jane shook her head. "I'm sorry, I don't understand.

Debra stopped still. "Oh dear. I was replaying our future conversation in my head. The conversation that I thought would come about in the next few seconds. When people visit, they ask me the same things and I thought that you were going to ask me too."

Jane couldn't help smiling. *"Ask you what?"*

"Why Jeremiah is still living at home. It's so weird, me saying that just now. You must think I'm odd. Have you ever done what I did just now?"

"Nee. I don't think I have, but it sounds like it would be an easy thing to do."

"You're kind, Jane. It was a mistake, and it might've been an easy mistake to make, but I have to separate what goes on in my head and what happens in the real world."

That comment startled Jane. She too would have to do that.

"You see, I have Jeremiah, my oldest, living at home

and it bothers me. That's probably why I'm thinking about it all the time and it's also what people ask me about when they're looking to have a conversation. Because you've just come to say hello, you'll get around to talking about my *kinner,* sooner or later."

"You're so right, Debra. That's very true. So, he's still living at home?"

Debra sighed deeply. *"Jah,* he is."

"And you'd rather him not be here?"

"I'd rather him be married, Jane. Married and giving me *grosskin."*

"He'll get there when the time is right." Jane grinned. Everybody was always telling her that, so she took every opportunity to repeat it to as many people as she could. For her, the right time was always now. She would never share her inner thoughts with anyone, but sometimes it seemed that *'Gott's* timing,' never happened.

"Can I come in?" Isaac called out from the next room.

"Come in, Isaac. We're in the kitchen."

Isaac walked in and sat down.

"What would you like, Isaac, hot tea or *kaffe?"*

"I wouldn't mind a coffee. I like the way you make it."

"Denke. And for you, Jane?"

"Just a black tea for me, weak and no sugar for a change."

"That's easy enough. Isaac, we were just talking about Jeremiah."

"Jah, I was having a good talk with Jeremiah last night."

"Were you indeed?"

"Yes."

"Did he happen to mention any young ladies?"

"Are you asking me whether he might be interested in someone?"

"That's exactly what I'm asking. All I wanted him to do is get married. He doesn't even have to leave this *haus,* he can get married and move his *fraa* right on in. We'll make room. It's a big *haus,* plenty of space."

"You'll be pleased to know that he does like someone. But don't ask me any more because I can't tell you."

"That's all I wanted to know."

Jane giggled. "You men and your secrets."

"Don't women have secrets?"

"They're nothing like men's secrets," said Debra.

"Women gossip, and men don't," Isaac stated.

"Certain men do, Isaac," Debra said. "I can guarantee you that. I get to hear many things. Not that I eavesdrop, but my ears can't stop hearing."

Isaac and Jane exchanged a smile. Debra was certainly entertaining.

When she'd made the hot tea and the coffee, she sat down with them, placing a bowl of sugar cookies on the table. "Now, what have you two got planned today?"

Jane had no idea and she looked at Isaac, who said, "Jane can show me around. We didn't get much time last time we went out."

"Which was yesterday," Jane commented.

"Yes. Jane couldn't spare me much time. Now we have the whole day together."

"That sounds lovely and what will you show him, Jane?"

"I'm not sure yet. We haven't really talked about what he'd like to do."

"It doesn't really matter what we do. It'll be nice to spend some uninterrupted time with her."

Jane took a cookie and bit into it. Spending so much time with Isaac, she was certainly seeing a different side to him—a far more controlling side. He was different when he was at home.

Was this the man God had for her? It was hard to imagine it was, because she wasn't looking forward to spending the entire day with him. And if spending a day with him seemed tiresome, how would she handle spending her entire life with him?

It was a whole hour later when they left the bishop's house.

"That took a long time," said Isaac as they traveled down the bishop's driveway to get back onto the road.

"I know. She can talk."

185

"You should've excused us sooner. You know I wanted to spend all day with you. I just thought we'd be there for fifteen minutes. I didn't know you were going to accept hot tea which turned into a full blown morning tea with food."

Jane pressed her lips together. She felt like a schoolgirl getting berated by her teacher. "I always accept the offer to eat when someone invites me."

"That would be fine if you were alone, but you could've checked with me first."

"Sorry, Isaac. I'll do that in future."

He glanced over at her. "I'm sorry, Jane. You must think I'm awful. I'm just so uptight."

"What about?"

"About losing you. I know Matt is interested in you and that's why you're here."

"I can tell you that I'm here for a very different reason."

He held up his hand. "Don't lie to me."

Jane was taken aback by the comment. It was so abrupt. "I'm not. I wouldn't. It's true."

"Is it?" Isaac stared at her.

She swallowed hard wondering if he would guess *her* reason for being there was that she was in love with Matt, even though Matt's reason was something else entirely. She didn't want Isaac to know either of them.

CHAPTER 23

"It is."

He smiled and looked back at the road. "Tell me where I'm going. I want to go somewhere we won't be interrupted by people you know."

"I should've packed us a picnic and we could've eaten it in the park."

"Perfect, a picnic."

"But it's too late for that, unless you want to go back to Sadie's."

"*Nee.* We can get takeout burgers and fries and sit in the park."

It seemed to Jane that he liked burgers and fries. That was what they'd had the day before. "That sounds *wunderbaar.* I know the perfect place to get food like that and there's a park by the river a two minute drive from there." What she didn't tell Isaac was that Matt's produce store was close to the fast food burger restaurant.

When they drove past it twenty minutes later, she had a good look and saw Matt's horse and buggy out behind the building. If only she was spending the day with Matt and not her uptight neighbor from back home. Still, she was prepared to give Isaac a chance. It was the least she could do after he'd come all that way to see her. He'd gone to so much trouble.

They drove through the drive-through, one of only two in the district that could fit a horse and buggy.

Once they had their food, they continued on to the picnic area.

Isaac found a blanket in the back of the buggy and they spread it out and then placed all their food on it. "The only thing that ruins this day is that it's so chilly."

"It's not too bad. I don't mind the cold."

"Well, you can't feel it like I do if you say you don't mind it."

"That might be right. I could have a higher internal temperature than other people." Or it could've been the double layers of thermal underwear she always wore under her dresses in the wintertime, but she wasn't going to tell him that.

He tilted his face to the sky. "It's miserable."

She looked up at the dark gray sky that was scattered with clouds. "It's not. I have to disagree. It's a beautiful blue gray, such lovely tones. *Gott* is an artist, don't you think so? Look at all the different colors and hues. Then He breathed in deeply, and slowly, calmly, blew the clouds across the sky."

He looked up with his mouth open. "You're right, Jane. It is pretty spectacular. I never stopped to admire the sky, not the way you did just now."

"I always look for beauty everywhere. There's beauty in all things. We just have to know how to see it."

"When I'm looking at you, I don't have to learn how to see it."

She giggled at him being so corny. He was trying hard to give her a compliment. *"Denke,* Isaac. That's a lovely thing to say."

"It's true. You are a true beauty, Jane, inside and out."

She looked down and blushed.

"Now, let's eat." He was quickly distracted by the food, but Jane was pleased he'd taken the time to say nice things to her. She seldom heard such things. He unwrapped her burger and then his. "I know this is not grand, and you deserve a better meal than this, but …"

"Nee. It's perfect."

He smiled and then bit into his burger.

Jane continued, "It's perfect to be among nature and the trees with the water just over there. It's nicer than sitting in a building to eat. I've been to a few restaurants before and it's not as good as eating in the outdoors or in someone's home."

"Mm, I'm with you there. I'd much rather eat and have fellowship in a brother's home."

Jane didn't think she could take a bite without making a mess, so she ripped off some of the burger with the bun and popped it into her mouth.

"You must miss Rosalee," Jane said when she had finished her mouthful.

"I do. Every minute I'm away from her."

"I'm missing her too," said Jane. "I'm used to seeing her every evening when I get home."

"I'm sorry about that. You get home when I'm finishing off the milking. I've told her to stay indoors and leave you be."

"I've told you that's fine. I enjoy our talks. Where is she staying?"

"With her *grossmammi*."

"*Jah*, that's right. You told me that. That's good. They'll have fun together."

"I wrote to her as soon as I got here. I told her what it was like and about the trip on the Greyhound. She's never been on a Greyhound bus before."

"You'll have so much to tell her when you get home."

He smiled at her. "Do you think so?"

As soon as she realized he had taken what she said

the wrong way, she didn't know what to do. All she could do was nod politely.

When they had finished their food, he tossed their rubbish into the trashcan and then folded up the blanket and they walked back to the buggy where he carefully replaced the blanket. "Would you like to go for a walk?"

"I was just going to suggest that."

"Good. We think alike, and I agree with you now."

She looked over at him. "What about?"

"It is a beautiful day even if it is a little cold and gray."

"I'm glad you think so. What a boring world it would be if we had sunshine or rainbows every day. We need the dark and we need the light to shine in the dark." Jane laughed at her own words.

"You make me happy, Jane. I want that for myself and Rosalee. Even just the few minutes she's with you of an evening has enriched her life."

His words made her feel good and she knew he was speaking from his heart. She was glad she could be a good presence in someone's life. "I hope so."

"She misses having a mother like all her friends, and I'm sure the time spent with you makes up for that in some way."

"Thank you. That's a lovely thing to say."

"You remind *me* of her."

Now things were getting a little awkward. "Oh, I didn't know."

"It's not a bad thing. In fact, it could be seen as a good thing."

"Um, yes it could be a good thing. That's how I took it to be."

"I hope you've given some thought to the question I asked you before."

Jane nodded. "I have. I've been giving it some serious thought."

"You don't have to give me your answer just yet. I know you wouldn't have had much time to think about it."

"Good." Jane was longing to get back to Sadie's place.

"I'm a patient man. I can wait."

"It's good to know."

"I don't want to wait too long."

Jane stopped walking and looked at him. "I don't understand. You just said you were patient."

"Are you patient?" he asked.

"I am."

"Jane, I love—"

"Don't say it," Jane blurted out before she started walking quickly to the water.

He followed after her. "I do."

Jane had never been more uncomfortable. She threw a quick glance over her shoulder hoping no one was around to see them walking together, and misinterpret their relationship.

At that moment, the wind swept up and he looked up into the sky. "I think it's going to rain. Look how those rain clouds have come over."

"Nee, I don't think it's going to rain." As she too looked up in the sky, little sprinkles fell on her nose and cheeks. "Oh, I think that *was* rain."

"Let's go." He grabbed her arm, swiveling her toward the buggy. Then he walked with her, fast. "I dislike getting caught out in the rain, and it happens to me so often. And it's so easy for me to catch a cold."

"I'm used to the weather around these parts. It's not going to end up in a storm or anything."

"Are you sure?"

"Yes, I think it's just those few little sprinkles and that will be it. It could rain later tonight. This time of year, it doesn't usually rain in the afternoon."

"I'll have to take your word on that." He slowed his pace and let go of her arm, while he asked, "Are you cold?"

"I'm fine."

"Because if you're cold I could take my coat off and give it to you."

She giggled. "You've only just finished telling me that you catch colds easily."

"I'll be fine," he growled.

"I just don't want you to be uncomfortable."

"I'm truly okay."

Just as she was about to suggest they turn back, the sky grew darker and the heavens opened, and the rain pour down. He grabbed her and pulled her under a tree, but it wasn't much shelter from the rain. It was still pouring through the branches.

"We'll have to head back to the buggy." He took off his coat and made a shelter over both of them as they made a dash back to the buggy.

Jane had realized their walk had taken them so far.

When they eventually got back into the buggy, he wiped the water off his face. "I'm drenched."

"Me too," she said taking off her black over-bonnet, which was thoroughly soaked by now.

He looked at her with a sour face. "You told me it wouldn't rain like that."

"I didn't think it would. It's not the typical weather pattern here."

He took hold of the reins. "Time to head back, and I just hope I don't catch a cold."

"Maybe there are towels in the buggy somewhere so we can dry off."

"*Nee,* they only had the blanket. What did you think, they keep towels in the buggy in case they want to go for a swim?"

She knew he was upset over being caught in the rain, but did he have to be so sarcastic towards her? She remained silent, regretting having said it wouldn't rain. The buggy was an old one and didn't have a heater in it so by the time they got to Sadie's house, they were both shivering from being in their damp clothes.

"Do you want to stop here and see if Sadie might have some of Matt's or her other sons' clothes tucked away somewhere? It's another fifteen to twenty minutes to the bishop's house."

"I'll be fine. Forgive me if I don't get out and walk you into the house, Jane."

"That's quite alright. Are you sure you won't —"

"Just get out of the buggy, Jane," he said through gritted teeth.

Jane was taken aback and quickly got out of the buggy and because it was still raining, she ran to the house.

Sadie opened the door and looked horrified. "Jane! You're all wet."

Jane burst out crying and fell into Sadie's outstretched arms. She sobbed on Sadie's shoulder for what felt like a good five minutes.

"Whatever is the matter?" Sadie eventually asked. "Let's get you out of these wet clothes, shall we?"

"I'll change. Oh dear, I'm sorry, now I've made you all wet too."

"It's okay." Sadie walked to the cupboard and pulled out a large fluffy towel. "Dry yourself, get out of those wet clothes, and I'll heat you up some soup."

"*Denke,* Sadie," Jane sniffled. She'd had a terrible

day. She had tried to talk herself into liking Isaac, but he had shown underlying anger the whole time.

After Jane took off her wet clothes, she arranged them on a hanger and hung them by the window to dry. Then she dried herself with a towel and pulled on some dry clothes. Her hair and prayer *kapp* were dry, thanks to her over-bonnet that had absorbed most of the water.

Once she had pushed her dry-stockinged feet into a pair of dry shoes, she collected her wet apron and stockings, and headed out the door to find Sadie in the living room.

"Where shall I put these, Sadie?"

Sadie jumped to her feet. "I'll take them from you. You sit in front of the fire. I'll put these in the laundry room and we can worry about them tomorrow."

Jane moved to warm herself in front of the crackling fire. It was nice to be all warm and toasty again.

In a minute, Sadie was back with a bowl of steaming pea and ham soup.

"This was to be for dinner. It still can be if you don't mind eating it again tonight."

"Oh, I love pea and ham soup. My *mudder* used to make it all the time."

When Jane had eaten the last spoonful, she became aware that Sadie had been watching her the whole time. Jane cleared her throat. "I suppose you're wondering why I was upset."

"Because you were soaked through to the skin?"

Jane shook her head. *"Nee.* It was because of Isaac. He wasn't very nice. He seemed angry all the time. He said things that weren't very nice. And don't ask me what, because it was nothing in particular."

"That's okay you don't have to explain anything. Men can be difficult sometimes."

Jane sighed. "Then he said some nice things too. Some lovely things about me. Oh, I shouldn't have said such mean things about him. He came all this way for me so I thought I should give him a chance. He seems so different when he's at home." Jane wiped a tear from her eye as a mixture of emotions swam in her head.

"I'm sorry, Jane. It can't be easy for you." Sadie leaned forward. "What did he do to upset you?"

"Nothing. Everything. Not much, really." She shook her head. *"Ach. Denke* for the soup. It was lovely."

"So, you won't be marrying him?"

"Nee. I won't. Today has made that quite clear to me."

"Have you told him that yet?"

Jane opened her mouth, and then realized she should've told him. Although, she couldn't see when, given the rain and his stressed-out behavior. "I guess I've got a lot to think about," Jane mumbled as she looked into the flames of the fire.

"Maybe you need to talk to a friend? What if I see if Jessica can stop by tomorrow?"

"*Jah.* I'd love that. *Denke.*"

Even the thought of telling Isaac 'no' made her feel uncomfortable, she didn't want to hurt his feelings.

Also … she needed someone to marry when Matt married someone else, didn't she?

CHAPTER 24

THE NEXT DAY, Jessica arrived to talk to Jane. While Sadie entertained her two granddaughters in the living room, Jane and Jessica sat in the kitchen having a serious conversation over coffee.

"Forget everything about feelings and such. What you've got to do is tell him it's over," Jessica told Jane regarding Isaac.

"It's hard. I like him as a person. But I don't think I'd be happy living with him. He's too bossy and angry."

"You want Matt, right?"

"*Jah,* always have."

"Let's think about this. He sees you as a friend, right?"

Jane nodded. "Most definitely."

"How has he reacted when Isaac came here?"

Jane thought about his reaction. "He doesn't like it."

"Hmm. He's jealous. What you've got to do is make out you're as popular as he is."

"Ach, I couldn't do it. No one would ever believe it."

Jessica laughed. "All you need is for Matt to believe it. Now, he had five women he was considering …"

"Only three now."

"Whatever. So what you need is to pretend there are a few men wanting to marry you."

Jane giggled at the thought. "Would he ever believe it?"

"Ach Jah! You're beautiful, Jane, and such a nice person. I'm surprised you're not married by now but that's only because you never got over Matt."

Jane thought about what Jessica was asking her to do. "I can't do that. It would be a lie."

"Nee, it wouldn't. You've got Isaac who's interested in you, even asked you to marry him, and surely there's someone else you might be interested back in your community."

"Not really."

"Think hard. How many single men are there?"

"Well, of all the ones over twenty-five, who are anywhere near my age, there would be three unmarried and I'm not counting all the old, old men."

Jessica wasn't about to give up. "Out of those you mentioned, who would be the best one?"

"I guess that would be Kevin Perdy."

"Perfect and if you were interested in him, do you think he would be interested in you?"

"I guess so. *Jah*, I think he would be."

"So tell Matt you have two men you're choosing between. He'll believe it because one even chased you over here."

Jane considered it, and then shook her head. She'd never been comfortable with lying. "It's stretching the truth and it doesn't sit well with me. I feel I would be deceiving him and I don't want to do that."

"Neither do I, but we need him to see that you have options as well and you're not just his 'single friend with no hope' he's asking advice from. We need him to see you as a possible choice."

It still bothered Jane that she wasn't his only choice, and that was the way things should've been. "I don't know if I could do it. He'd know I was lying. I mean, how would I tell him about this fake other man? How would that come up in conversation?"

"Tell him ... tell him that you like his idea and you also have decided to marry before this Christmas."

Jane put her hand over her mouth and giggled. Her friend always made her feel better. "You're so funny, Jessica."

"Hey, there's nothing funny about it. Do you want him or not?"

"I do, but I want him to want me."

Jessica banged her fist on the table causing Jane to jump. "That's just your ego talking. You want him, yet you want it to be how you always pictured it. Well it's never going to be how you pictured it, is it? Otherwise, you would've been married to him ten years ago!"

She stared at Jessica and realized she was right. "I do want him no matter what."

"Good. Now, do exactly what I say."

By this time, Jane was willing to do anything to be happily married to Matt.

THAT NIGHT when Matt came for dinner, Sadie disappeared from the kitchen saying she was having an early night. Of course, Jane had asked Sadie to do just that.

"I hope *Mamm's* all right. She's not sick or anything, is she?" Matt asked.

"*Nee*. She didn't sleep well last night, so she's just catching up on some sleep."

"Ah, good."

"I need to ask you something, Matt."

He smiled. "Sounds serious."

"It is. When you make your choice, could you spare some time to do the same for me?"

His eyebrows drew together. "What's that?"

"Come and visit my community, and help me choose a man."

His mouth opened but no words came out. Eventually, he said, "You want to get married?"

"Of course I do."

"I just thought that you …"

"I don't have as many as you to choose from. I only have two men who want to marry me. It's so difficult to choose, that's why I stayed to help you. I understand how daunting it can be. I had more than two, but I've ruled out the others and I'm down to two."

"I do appreciate it. *Jah,* I'll do whatever I can to help you like you've done for me."

"Just wait until next year. After you're married. You and your *fraa* can stay with my neighbors. They're good friends of mine."

His mouth twitched at the corners. "Tell me about these men."

"Oh, there's nothing much to tell. Both so nice, so hard working. They're both more than I could ever have asked for. *Gott* has blessed me. Isaac is one of them."

Slowly, he nodded. "You've never married or talked about being married until now. And at your age… well, I thought you would've married by now if you wanted that life."

"I guess we've never discussed that part of our lives." A giggle escaped her lips. "I'm not sure why."

"Me neither."

"It's up to you of course, but I think Marcy is the

one who suits you perfectly fine. She's fun and lively and I've heard she's such a good cook."

"Marcy?"

Jane nodded enthusiastically.

"That's funny. I thought you would've chosen someone else."

"*Nee*. Marcy. The younger the woman the more likely you'll be to have loads of *kinner*. She's not the youngest, but I still think she suits you fine."

He frowned. "I'm not choosing a woman based on how many children she can give me."

"Marry someone my age and you won't have as many."

He rubbed his jaw. "I never thought of that."

"Well, you have to think of these things. It's only being practical."

"I'm happy with whatever number of *kinner Gott* decides to give me."

She nodded, pleased with that answer.

"What about love, though?" he asked.

"Love?"

A smile lit up his face. *"Jah."*

"I can't help you with that part. Only you know the true feelings in your heart. There's no way I can tell you what you feel."

He drew in a deep breath. "I've got a lot of thinking to do."

"I hope I'm not putting you under too much pressure with helping me choose a husband?"

"*Nee.* Not at all. I'll look forward to it."

Jane smiled as though she didn't have a care in the world. *"Kaffe?"*

"*Jah,* please." As Jane got up to make the coffee, he said, "I know you've got Isaac here to see you, but could you spare the day with me tomorrow?"

"Okay. I explained to Isaac I was here to help you with something—he doesn't know what it is. He's okay with only getting small bits of my time."

"Good."

As she filled the teakettle, she glanced over at him. He was looking down at the table, deep in thought as he traced and retraced the wood grain with a fingertip.

CHAPTER 25

As soon as Matt brought Jane to his place the next day, he asked the question, "What do you think of the twins?"

She stepped out of the buggy and joined him, and together they headed to the house. "I already told you what I think about them."

Was that the only reason he asked her to spend the day there with him? Or maybe to give him ideas on how to make the place nice for his new bride? She had hoped that he wanted to spend time with her, get to know his old friend again in person rather through their letters. She stared at him.

He arched an eyebrow. "So…?"

"Oh, the twins."

"*Jah*. Refresh my mind about what you think of them."

Was he having second thoughts about one of them? Perhaps he was in love with one of them and didn't want them dismissed so easily. "Although they don't really look that much alike, their personalities are very similar. If you're asking me to choose between them, I can't. I simply can't. Unless … unless there is something about one of them that you prefer over the other. If there is I can't see what it might be." She did see. One was tall like her and the other was short. And he certainly wasn't attracted to her. Would he prefer, Beatrice, the shorter of the twins?

He looked away. *"Jah,* they are similar. That's a hard problem."

"They are both lovely to look at."

"I thought you might see something in one of them that the other didn't have."

"Nee, sorry. I can't help you out with that one."

"Do you see one of them as more suited to me than say .. Marcy or Lanie?"

She screamed in her head, *Don't you see me? Am I invisible to you?*

When she didn't say anything, he suggested, "Let's take a walk around outside shall we?"

"Okay." She cleared her throat and did her best to rid her head of self-pity. "So far, I think the person you are most suited with is Marcy. She's at a good age."

"Age shouldn't come into it."

"Well not age, but maturity, life experience." She

saw his lips twitch. "Don't you want someone who is on a similar mental mindset as yourself?"

"It might be refreshing to have someone younger, to keep me younger in the head. I never want to become old in my thinking."

She felt that sting as though he'd slapped her across the face. He clearly wanted someone younger, someone who could give him many *kinner*. At just over thirty years of age the number of children she could give him was limited simply by the late start that she'd have.

She desperately wanted to get out of there, but she'd made a commitment and she was a person of her word. That kept her there no matter how painful, no matter how hard. "Is that what we're going to be doing all day, talking about your five prospects?"

He chuckled. "I wish you'd stop calling them prospects."

"Well they are prospects. Contenders. Contestants."

"You have two as well."

"*Jah,* but two is not five. Do they know that I'm screening them for you?" She'd found out that Lanie knew.

He chuckled again. This time he appeared embarrassed, as he took off his hat and smoothed his hair back. She knew all his mannerisms and what they meant. "One or two of them might have an idea. I might have mentioned something."

"Lanie would've guessed. She seems the most switched on out of any of them."

"You might be right about that."

But it appeared he didn't want a bright woman, or a woman he could converse with. He as good as said he wanted a younger woman he could protect and who could give him loads of children.

As they walked, she looked over at him and tried to make herself dislike him, loathe him even. It would be so much easier if she could lose her feelings or at least hide them away until she got back home to her community.

What was wrong with her that he didn't love her? Surely it was more than her looks.

Maybe he didn't want someone who had been a friend. He had loads of friends.

"Let's put the women out of our heads today. We could both do with not thinking about them for a day."

"I think that's a good idea."

As he talked about the property, they walked towards the river, where they used to play as children. He talked about his plans for the improvements on the property and the different crops he was going to try.

"So, you're not going to lease the land to one of your brothers?"

"I might when I turn the place into a bed and breakfast. Everything is up in the air at the moment."

Jane was feeling so sorry for herself she wasn't

even listening about corn and soybeans and whatever other crops he was chattering about. She walked slowly along looking at the earth beneath her change colour.

"It's been dry this year," she said when he paused for breath.

"It has been. We're having a dry spell."

Hmm, she thought, *much like my life.* "Hopefully next year will be better."

She smiled and looked around. "I've always loved this place. Remember how we used to play along the banks of the river and hide in the trees when we were younger?"

"Those are some of my fondest memories of my childhood." He gave her a beaming smile.

"If only people didn't need to grow up. Things were so simple back when I was a young girl and my parents and siblings were still here. I didn't have to worry about one single thing except getting our chores done on time." She'd felt so alone once her brother and sister had gone. They had both left at the same time without a trace and they'd tried to get her to go with them. She wouldn't hear of it.

"And doing exactly what we were told," he added.

"*Jah,* that too. Things are so uncertain when you become an adult. When I was growing up, I had so many different dreams for my future. It seemed that anything was possible."

"What kind of things? Get married and have a family? Isn't that what every woman wants?"

"*Jah,* that's right. Within that framework is what I used to dream of."

His eyebrows pinched together. "I'm not sure I understand."

She couldn't tell him that she used to think of being married to him. "What my *kinner* would be like and … and who I would marry, and so on."

"Oh." He looked away. When they came to a large outcrop of rocks, he sat down on one of them. "Tell me about the dreams you used to have."

She sat on one too. "Nothing definite, just whether I'd get married in the afternoon or the morning, and where my husband and I would live."

"Ah, I guess that's changed now since you moved away."

"I never thought I'd be gone indefinitely."

"You didn't?"

She shook her head. *"Nee."*

"Why did you move?"

"I was upset about my brother and sister leaving. You know, they've never kept in touch. I've not heard one word from them since they left." She wiped a tear from her eye.

"I'm sorry, Jane. That must be so hard for you."

"It is. It was bad enough our folks dying, and then they both disappeared, left me with no one."

"I had no idea that was how you felt." He moved off his rock, sat next to her and put his arm around her. "I'm so sorry, Jane. I guess I got caught up in my own life and never realized how much you were hurting."

She wiped more tears from her cheeks. "It's okay. I just miss them. I think about them every day. They probably have families by now. And, how do I know they're still alive? Something might've happened to them and I'd never know."

"That's why you left?"

"Partly. I honestly don't know what I want."

"What about your suitors back home?"

She shook her head. "I don't know what will happen there. Maybe I'll marry one of them, and maybe I won't. You see? There are so many choices now. As a child there are no maybes, no choices, there were just definite ideas of what would happen."

He held her tighter. "If life could be anything you want … how many *kinner* would you see yourself with?"

That brought a smile to her face. "I always thought six was the perfect number. Three boys and three girls. Three would be boys, first, and the second lot of three would be the girls. They would all stay within the community, not one of them would leave like my siblings did."

"You never heard anything from either of them?"

"*Nee*, you're the first person to mention them to me in years. I don't even know where they are. They

213

haven't tried to contact me either, and it wouldn't be too hard to find out where I live. They'd only need to ask Bishop David. He has my address."

"Yes, you're right. It wouldn't be too hard. Sorry about that."

"Don't be sorry, that's just the way things are. These things happen. I didn't want them to stay if they didn't want to. I know, and I knew then, that they have to follow what they think is right in life."

"Are you going to stay where you're living forever?"

"I don't know. I don't need to. What are your plans, Matt? Marry one of these women and turn your *haus* into a bed and breakfast?"

"I won't ask you about which man you'll choose because you don't seem to know that."

"And because that part is not up to me. I need your help." She smiled sweetly. Jessica would be proud of her. This was developing just like they'd planned. He was bothered by talk of her marrying.

"I'll do all I can to help."

"After you've made your choice, and after you're married," she said.

"*Jah,* of course."

She looked up at the sky. "It's gray again. I hope we don't get rained on."

He grinned. "I like the rain."

His attitude was so different from Isaac's, and she was glad. And, he still had his arm around her ...

CHAPTER 26

AFTER MATT finally took Jane back to his mother's in the mid-afternoon, he went straight to Lanie's house and banged on the door.

She opened it, staring at him. "What's wrong?"

He pushed right on past her into the house. "Our plan is not working. She's got this new man, Isaac. Now she's informed me, she has a second man back home." He turned around to face her, his skin flushed scarlet. "And she wants me to help her choose between them. ME!" He pointed to himself. "Our plan has back-fired badly."

"I met Isaac and he seems to be a lovely man."

"So, can you see my concern? If they're in love, I won't stand in the way of her happiness."

"I don't think that's a problem."

"Why do you say that?"

"Leave it with me. I'll find out exactly how he feels about her."

"And how would you do that? Have you gotten close enough to Jane in the short amount of time she's been back? I can't see her telling you how she really feels. She's very closed off with people she doesn't know. She's quite a shy woman. Or maybe 'reserved' is a better word."

"Just trust me. I'll find out."

He took off his hat and ran a hand through his dark hair. "I regret doing this now. I pulled her all the way over here for nothing. I've embarrassed myself. I'm sure she thinks I'm a fool. A big fool."

"Just give it a chance. Don't give up just yet."

He swallowed hard. "Are you sure you can find out? What am I thinking? He chased her all the way over here. I should've been man enough to do that myself years ago."

"I'm positive I can find out what I need from him." Lanie felt the burden of the foolish plan to rid his mind of Jane. Now she knew how sick he was over the possibility of losing her, and she realized how deep his love was. There was no way she could compete. The whole 'Jane choosing his bride' had been her idea even though Matt was trying to take responsibility for it. It had seemed perfect when they'd first talked about it, but now she could see it hadn't been a great idea. Not even a mediocre one. "Leave it with me. I'll let you know."

EARLY THE NEXT DAY, Lanie stopped by the bishop's house hoping to see Isaac.

She had no idea what she was going to say, but she knew she had to say something. She was sure there was a spark between herself and this man, and if there was, she couldn't allow him to marry Jane. What were the chances of two men she liked being in love with Jane?

Debra, the bishop's wife opened the door after Lanie knocked. "Lanie, how nice to see you. Where's Mary-Lee?"

"I just dropped her off with my mother."

"I always enjoy seeing her. Come in."

She walked through the doorway. "Well, *denke,* but I'm actually here to see Isaac if he's in."

"Isaac's helping mend one of our boundary fences. I overheard the men say it was two hundred yards up on the northern side."

"Do you mind if I go and talk to him?"

"If you wish."

"Okay thanks. I'll go see him."

The bishop's wife shut the door and Lanie walked along the fence line, looking between the trees to see if she could catch sight of him. When she walked up a slight rise, she saw him, working by himself, and another man working another fifty yards away. She hurried to Isaac, seizing the opportunity to talk to him by himself.

He looked up and saw her approaching. Then he straightened up and smiled. "Hello, Lanie. What are you doing out this way?"

"I was just taking a walk."

"Is that right? Taking a walk on the bishop's property?"

"Guilty," she said fluttering her dark eyelashes. "I did want to talk to you."

He put the hammer down on the ground and his hands dropped by his sides. "About what?"

"I want to let you know that I've enjoyed our conversations." She could see when he smiled that he wasn't totally focused on Jane above all other women. Unlike Matt who'd never once looked at her the way Isaac was right now. "It would be nice if you could visit this community more often."

He crossed his arms over his chest looking slightly embarrassed. "I would if I had a reason. It's not easy for me to get away from my goats."

"I just love goats."

"Yes, you mentioned that before. I remembered."

"I hope you found someone good to look after them in the end."

"I did. My sister's husband. He'd offered many times to look after them. He helps me a few hours a week so he knows what to do. He's really the only one I'd trust."

"Sounds like you're a very tough man when it comes to giving someone your trust."

He smiled. "Sometimes. I'm glad I came here."

"Things are working out for you here?"

He gave a lopsided grin. "They're looking better."

She giggled. "How so?" She touched the fence and he grabbed her hand.

"Careful, I haven't fixed that yet." His fingers lingered, curled around her hand, before he slowly released it.

His caress was so caring, so gentle. She looked into his eyes, and something passed between them. Something unknown, unspoken, and what's more, they both knew that the other knew it.

"If I hadn't come I never would've met you, Lanie."

"You feel that way?" she asked breathlessly.

"I sure do." He glanced over his shoulder at the other man working on the fence. Then he turned his attention back to Lanie. "How can I see more of you while I'm here?"

"I'm glad you said that." She had a quick decision to make. She'd fought her attraction to him because she knew he'd only come there for Jane. "Is there any chance you'll be home tonight at the bishop's *haus?* I'll be there for the quilting bee. We go every Tuesday."

"I'll make sure I'm there. The bishop hasn't

mentioned that he's wanted me to do anything tonight."

"Good. The men usually stay in the kitchen while we take over the living room, but we'll have a chance to talk over a late supper."

"Will we?" he asked.

"We will."

"I'll look forward to it."

"As will I. I'll see you tonight then, Isaac."

"I'll be there, waiting."

Lanie walked away, feeling like she'd never felt before. Was there a chance for her? A chance for her daughter to have a father in Isaac? A sister in his daughter Rosalee?

CHAPTER 27

LANIE WASN'T GOING to get her hopes up just yet. Yes, they'd had a moment where it felt like they were the only two on Earth, but that meant nothing if he didn't profess his love or give her some hope to cling to. What she needed was for him to promise he'd return, or for him to invite her to his own community in Holmes County. If he did that, she could be sure their relationship would develop quickly.

Her chance to talk to him again came at the late supper that night at the bishop's house. The two of them slipped out onto the chilly porch so they could speak in private.

"I've never met anyone quite like you, Lanie."

She felt the same, but the question had to be asked. "What about Jane?"

"Jane's not interested in me. I can tell she's in love with someone else."

"Oh, are you certain?"

"I was going to go home tomorrow unless … if you want me to stay on a couple more days, I could."

"Please stay, Isaac."

"I will, then. Can you get to the main farmers market in town tomorrow by ten?"

"I'll make sure I'm there."

"Good. We should get back inside now, before we're missed."

"Okay," she said as she went to walk in, but he suddenly pulled her back.

"Lanie, I came here to get myself a *fraa* and it seems that's what I'm doing, if you'll do me the honor."

"Isaac, do you really mean it?"

"Will you marry me, Lanie?"

She licked her lips. This was what she wanted. They didn't really know each other, but somehow she felt that they did. Some might say that it was madness, but Lanie felt in her heart that it was right. "I will, Isaac, I will."

He pulled her into his arms.

"Wait. I'm thinking about Jane."

"If Jane and I had been right for one another, we would've got together a long time ago. I know that because I can see things clearly now. Now that I've met you."

Lanie was smiling so much, her face ached. She felt like she hadn't stopped smiling since she'd first met him.

"Would you leave your life here, marry me, and move Mary-Lee to Holmes County with me?"

"You truly mean it?"

He laughed. "If I didn't mean it, I wouldn't have said it."

Lanie didn't want to hurt Jane if she really loved Isaac. She had to find out first. "I'm worried how Jane will take this. You came to see her and now you've proposed to me."

"Jane's not interested in me and it's just as well she didn't give me an answer."

Lanie bit her lip. "Give me a couple of days, will you? I want to make sure Jane will be okay. I couldn't bear to see her hurt over this."

"You're such a caring person, Lanie."

Lanie was just being normal, she thought, but if he saw her as caring she wouldn't disagree. "I'll go see her tomorrow. I know that Sadie is going somewhere with the ladies, and I'm hoping Jane will be at Sadie's home all by herself."

"Then, will we be able to spend time together after that?"

"I'd love to, if all goes well. I'll see her tomorrow morning and then meet you at eleven. That'll give me plenty of time to talk with her woman-to-woman."

He gave her a nod.

THE NEXT MORNING OVER BREAKFAST, Sadie asked, "What are Matt's plans for you today, Jane?"

"He's very busy doing something at work. He said he's got some important meetings on. Looks like I've got a free day."

"Not any more. You can come with me to the charity meeting with the ladies."

Jane had been looking forward to a quiet day doing nothing. Since she'd arrived, she felt like she hadn't stopped. "Do you mind if I just stay home? I still haven't recovered from the trip over here."

"I don't mind at all, but you might enjoy coming with me, that's all."

"Any other time I would, but today I'd like to rest."

"If you feel the need to rest then that's what you should do. I know you're not a lazy woman and if your mind and your body are saying you need to rest then that's probably what you ought to do."

"*Denke* for understanding."

Just after nine, Sadie was collected by one of her friends, and Jane waved goodbye to them from the porch with Mr. Grover curled around her feet looking on. As soon as they drove away, Jane felt a great sense of relief.

She let out a deep breath. Then she relaxed onto the porch chair and wrapped her coat tighter around herself to keep out the chill of the morning air.

Mr. Grover wasted no time jumping onto her lap, helping to keep her warm. She patted him, burying her cold hands in his medium-length fur. "We have a whole day ahead of us, Mr. Grover. I'll have to make the evening meal, but I don't have to get started on that till around four. Sadie will be home at five. And all I want to do is … nothing." As the wind picked up, she added. "Maybe we should move to sit in front of the fire."

She carried Mr. Grover inside and shut the door behind them. She stood the cat on the floor, walked a few steps to the fire in the living room and rearranged the logs so they would burn slower and hotter. Then, after she added another couple of small logs, she sat down on the couch admiring her handiwork. Mr. Grover had already made himself comfortable on the rug and was fast asleep.

Jane stared into the flames, and she couldn't help thinking how funny life was. Life had taken various turns beyond her control and beyond anyone's control.

Here she was, back in the community where she'd grown up. Still, she couldn't help feeling alone. The old feelings she remembered from when her siblings deserted her returned. She missed having her family around. All she had in Holmes County were her extended family—aunts, uncles and cousins—but she wasn't that close with any of them.

Although, she realized, she did have a certain amount of control over her life. She had made the decision all those years ago to move to a different community.

After thirty minutes by herself, with the thought of the whole day stretched in front of her, she paced up and down in front of the fire wondering what to do with herself. She wasn't used to having free time apart from on Sundays.

Now she had nothing to do but think of Matt and what the outcome of his mission would be. Which woman would he marry and how much would he listen to her opinion?

After a full hour had dragged past, Jane was regretting her decision not to accompany Sadie. It might have been boring talking about their Christmas sewing projects, but it would've kept her mind off Matt.

Just as she was boiling the kettle to make herself a cup of coffee, she heard a horse and buggy. A spark of excitement fluttered inside her, and she hurried to look out the window hoping it was Matt. It was Lanie.

At that moment, Lanie was most welcome. She left the kitchen and opened the front door for her. "Hello, Lanie."

"Hi, Jane. Care for some company for an hour or so?"

"Sure. I'd love that. Come inside." When Jane saw Mary-Lee wasn't with her, she said, "You're fortunate to have your *mudder* look after Mary-Lee so often."

"Hmm, I haven't worked out if that's a good thing or a bad thing yet. What if she grows up thinking that my *mudder* is her *mamm?*"

Jane laughed. "I don't think that will happen. She's already five, you said."

"*Jah,* I suppose you're right. It is convenient sometimes."

"I just got the kettle boiling. Would you like a cup of coffee?"

"I brought chocolate cake, only I left it in the buggy."

"You brought some with you?"

"*Jah.*"

"Quick, go and get it! I could do with a piece of chocolate cake."

Lanie giggled at Jane, and hurried back out the door to the buggy.

Soon they were sitting down with a heavily frosted chocolate cake decorated with colored sprinkles, a sharp knife, plates and forks, and two cups of coffee.

"I'm glad you came here, Jane. I find you such an interesting person."

Jane was surprised. "Who me?"

"*Jah.* You're so brave. You moved away to another

community by yourself. I could never do that, all alone."

"I don't think it was brave. There was nothing left for me here after my folks died. I was on my own and I guess I wanted to see what else was out there, what life was like in other communities."

"And you had to start your life again."

Jane nodded as she pushed the knife through the cake. "It was a bit daunting at first, but everybody was very friendly. I made friends in no time and I still wrote to my old friends." Jane placed a slice of cake onto each of two plates.

"Denke," Lanie said pulling her plate of cake toward her and picking up a fork. "So do you think you might move back here in the future?"

"I don't know, depends what *Gott* has planned for me." She sipped her coffee. "Sometimes it's hard to make decisions."

"I think those are part of being human. We have to be sure to make the right ones, though, and some are life changing and some aren't that important."

"That's true. I'm glad you came today. I nearly went with Sadie to the ladies charity meeting."

"Ach." Lanie waved a hand through the air. "I never go to those things. I have my own sewing to do and I'm paid to do it. If I was old and didn't need the money to live on, I'd do it to pass the time."

"That's right, you're a seamstress."

"*Jah*. I sew night and day and that's why I'm not very interested in doing it in my spare time, if you see what I mean."

"I do. And I don't blame you. Otherwise, you'd be sewing all the time."

"That's right."

Mr. Grover walked into the kitchen and meowed loudly, then jumped into Lanie's lap.

Lanie bolted to her feet, and Mr. Grover landed on the floor. "I'm sorry but I don't like cats. I didn't hurt him, did I?"

"*Nee*, he was able to land on his feet." With a little smile, Jane watched Mr. Grover stalk out of the room, looking as though he was disgusted.

Lanie sat down and noticed Jane's expression. "Don't tell me you like cats."

"I love cats. I'm going to get one some day."

"That's your goal in life, is it, Jane—to get a cat?"

Jane giggled. It did sound perfectly ridiculous. "It is one of my goals. I always think that pets make a house feel more like home."

"I think children make a home. The laughter of children. I only wish that my husband and I had been able to have more than one."

"I'm sure you'll marry again and have more, if that's what you'd like."

"That's what I'm hoping. And that's why I want to have a talk with you so you could put in a good word for me with Matt." Lanie was fishing to see where Jane's heart lay.

Jane broke off a piece of chocolate cake with her fork. "Would that be fair? Wouldn't that give you an unfair advantage?"

"Phooey, I don't care about that. I can't see Matt really being interested in the twins or either of the others."

"I guess he just wants to get my opinion so he can assess things from a different viewpoint. The decision's up to him, you know that, don't you?"

"I do. Of course you wouldn't have the final say-so, but I know he will put a lot of store on your opinion. He respects you."

"That's good to know. Anyway, let's not talk about men."

Lanie was upset. That was all she was there to talk about.

"I should go soon anyway. *Mamm* has Mary-Lee with her while she hosts the charity thing at her house, and I know Mary-Lee will be non-stop with her chatter. I'll need to rescue her."

"Oh, the same one as Sadie's going to?"

"*Jah.*"

"Won't you stay for another cup of coffee?"

"Oh no. I should get going."

"Would you like to take the rest of the chocolate cake with you? Sadie doesn't like chocolate and I'm sure Mary-Lee would like a piece."

"Oh, if you don't mind I will take it with me, and I'm sure my mother wouldn't say no to a slice either."

Jane reached for the box the cake had come in, and placed what was left back inside.

Then Lanie stood up. "I've enjoyed our talk, Jane. It'd be nice if you move back here. Do you think you ever will?"

"I have no idea. My life is so ... up in the air. Sometimes I feel I have no roots anywhere."

"I hope you move here. Enjoy the rest of your day."

"I will, at least I'll try to."

Lanie walked through the door. "Me too. I'll try to."

Jane leaned against the doorframe and watched Lanie leave.

Lanie got into her buggy, picked up the reins, and realized she was totally confused by Jane. She moved her horse forward, and gave a little wave to Jane before the horse headed down the driveway. Jane said she had no roots, and that sounded to Lanie like she wasn't in love with anyone—not Isaac and not Matt.

Poor Matt, the feelings Jane once had for him were no more. Now all *she* could think about was Isaac. She wouldn't let him get away, not when he felt the same about her.

Her next stop was to meet him at the farmers

markets and tell him she would marry him. Now that she'd spoken to Jane, her conscience was totally clear.

CHAPTER 28

JANE CLOSED THE DOOR.

Alone, again.

She walked over to the fireplace, picked up a poker, and jabbed at the fire. Then she settled back into the couch feeling full of chocolate cake. She closed her eyes and drifted into a deep sleep.

An hour later, Jane woke and saw from the clock above the mantle that it was half past twelve.

It was time for lunch, but she wasn't hungry after those two pieces of chocolate cake and the coffee. It was too cold to go outside and wander around and she couldn't write letters because she only wrote letters to Jessica and Matt and they were right here.

When Sadie arrived at four, driven in Matt's buggy, Jane couldn't have been more pleased to see them. Matt must've collected Sadie from wherever the ladies were having their get-together. She opened the front door smiling, until she saw their faces.

"Is something wrong?" she asked when they got closer.

"We do have news," Sadie said.

"You haven't heard any 'news' yourself?" Matt asked.

Jane frowned. "About what?"

Sadie sighed and looked over at Matt. "She doesn't know."

"What is it?" Now Jane was worried.

"Let's all go inside and we'll tell you."

When they were all seated, Sadie said, "I was at Elsie's place."

"That's where the charity meeting was held?" Jane asked wondering if she'd already been told.

"*Jah*, that's right, Lanie's *mudder's*."

"Okay, go on. What happened?"

"Just as we were about to go, Lanie arrived with Isaac and they had a very odd announcement to make."

"About what?" Jane looked at Matt hoping he'd tell her. He looked away.

"Isaac …" Sadie's voice trailed off.

"Just tell me."

"It's okay, *Mamm*. I'll tell her. Isaac and Lanie are getting married."

Jane sprang to her feet. "It can't be. She was here this morning. We ate chocolate cake and talked about

.... Nothing in particular. *Nee.* It's not right. He asked me."

Sadie stood up. "I'm sorry, Jane. I need to lie down." Sadie patted her shoulder and then left the room.

"Are you okay?" Matt asked.

Jane didn't know how to answer. She opened her mouth but no words came out. This was the man she was going to consider marrying when Matt married someone, but now that option was gone. Soon, Matt would marry and there'd be no hope for her. Her mouth turned down at the corners and she couldn't stop the tears.

He moved toward her and wrapped his arms around her and she sobbed on his shoulder. In between her tears, she managed to say, "I'm sorry. I'm being so selfish. You might've been about to choose Lanie and now she's gone. It's all Isaac's fault. If only he hadn't come."

He smiled at her and pushed back some golden-red strands of hair that had fallen over her face. "I wasn't going to choose Lanie."

She put her head back onto his shoulder and sobbed some more. Jane was too upset about Isaac for Matt to tell her the truth.

He'd promised his mother this coming Christmas was going to be her best ever. The thing she wanted most was for him to marry. He'd let everyone down, most of all Jane. It was his fault that Isaac had come to this community and met Lanie. He wrapped his arms tightly around Jane, feeling her pain. "It's okay. It'll all be okay." All he could do was comfort her. If only she loved him as much as she'd loved Isaac.

"Let's sit over here." He guided her back to the couch. "I know this has all been a shock to you Jane, but I need to confess something to you."

She held her head. "I don't know if I can take any more surprises."

"Okay, I won't tell you."

"*Nee*. You have to tell me now that you've told me there's something to tell me."

He smiled at her. "I know I'm not Isaac, but I need to tell you... Jane, I've loved you all my life. When you left you broke my heart."

She stared at him not able to believe her ears. "Why didn't you ever say ..."

"I figured if you loved me you wouldn't have left. I thought long and hard about going to see you and telling you how I felt, but I couldn't bear the thought of a possible rejection. I knew that if you loved me you would've stayed."

"So, what are you saying? I don't understand. You love me?"

"I do, Jane."

"What was all this about me helping you choose a *fraa?*"

"Don't be angry. It was an elaborate ruse to get you back. I thought if you saw I was serious about marrying someone else, that might spark some jealousy in you. Or you might look at me with different eyes." He shook his head. "It was a silly idea. I know that now."

"I don't know why you didn't just come out and tell me."

"Fear. Plain old fear. Would you have rejected me, Jane, all those years ago?"

"*Nee.* I wouldn't have. You're the reason I left."

"Me?"

"*Jah.* We grew apart and I saw no hope. The only thing I could do was leave and see if you missed me." Jane held her head unable to believe what was going on. "What do these five women think?"

"They've been in on it the whole way along. Lanie even helped me refine the plan."

Jane shook her head. She wanted to be angry, but he had done all this because he loved her. "It was a crazy thing to do." Tears filled her eyes, but this time they were happy tears.

"Love has made me crazy."

"Love?"

"*Jah.* I'm in love with you, Jane. Since we were children. I always thought we'd marry, assumed it even. Then we grew apart. I thought you weren't interested and then you left me."

"It was you who showed no interest in me. A man should pursue a woman and not the other way around. I was waiting for you."

"What you say is right, but back then I was too scared, too nervous and I put it off. I've lived for the letters you sent every week."

"Me too. For yours, I mean."

He smiled and took her hand. "Do you mean, you feel the same?"

"I do," she said through her tears. "I don't think I was crying about Isaac. I was crying because of …"

"It doesn't matter. I never saw you with him. It didn't mean that I wasn't jealous. The first time I've ever had that emotion in my life." Then, he reached out his hand and she took hold of it. "Jane, will you marry me?"

She looked right into his eyes. Her heart pumped so hard she felt she was going to burst. This was all she'd ever wanted. Was it really happening, or was she going to wake up and realize it had all been a dream?

"What do you say, Jane?" he asked.

"I say … *jah*, I will marry you, Matt Yoder."

He laughed and pulled her to her feet, then he lifted her into his arms and swung her in a circle, as though she was as light as a feather. He placed her down and they looked into each other's eyes. "I love you, Jane, always have. Now, everything is right with me."

"That's something I've always wanted to hear because I love you, too, and I always have, too."

He lowered his head slowly until their lips touched.

Then he encircled his arms about her and held her close.

"I can't wait to start our lives together. I feel we've wasted so much time, when we could've been married already."

A giggle spilled out of Jane's lips. "I know what you mean."

"Let's tell my mother."

"She'll be so shocked. She's upset with you for having me here to help you choose a *fraa*."

"I know. She's made that quite clear. She'll be delighted to know the truth."

"I can't believe that all of this was made up. Mind you, I didn't think it made any sense."

He laughed. "It made no sense at all. I saw the disapproval on your face and I'm so glad you didn't turn around and leave on the next Greyhound out of town. That was when I saw there might be some hope for me."

"I thought about it. None of the women seemed a good match to me. Except maybe Marcy, or possibly Lanie. Now, Lanie's marrying Isaac."

"Maybe that's why we had to wait."

"What do you mean?"

"What other reason would Isaac have found to come here? If he never came, he never would've met Lanie."

"That's right. I never thought of that."

"Everything happens in *Gott's* timing and for His purpose."

"It used to annoy me so much when I heard people say that. I'm the kind of person who doesn't like to wait. It seemed I was the one who had to wait for things all the time. But now I know that He does answer prayers even if sometimes we have to wait a little longer."

"There's no more waiting for us, Jane. Let's get married as soon as we can. You will move back here, won't you?"

"I will. I never really wanted to leave."

"Does that mean … I can't believe it's all happening. I made crazy plans trying to jolt you into loving me. Trying to make you jealous, trying to make you think about me as a possible husband."

"You didn't need to do any of it." She took a deep breath. "I've always loved you and no one else."

The corners of his lips turned upward just slightly. "Not Isaac?"

She shook her head. "He's a neighbor and a friend. I don't know what he was thinking when I left, but there was certainly nothing between us, ever."

"Why did you move away from here? Tell me exactly what went through your head?"

"I was twenty-five, Matt. I don't know how you remember it. I felt there was nothing here for me. My parents were gone. My siblings were gone. You never looked twice at me back then."

"You might be right. I was focused on building up the produce business."

"Whatever you were doing, it didn't involve me."

"I was stupid. Senseless. Forgive me. I never meant to ignore you. I think I never expected you to leave."

"You had some girlfriends."

"Never."

"I saw you with Molly and Meredith Schultz."

He grunted. "I forgot about them. Their *bruder* asked me to show them some attention. I was never interested in either of them. I only had each of them in my buggy the once." He smiled at her. "You loved me back then, so long ago?"

"I always loved you."

"I wish I had known that back then. It seems that so much time has gone by, like water rushing under a bridge. We can't stop the rushing water, but maybe we can jump in the river and see where it takes us."

"As long as you're by my side I'm willing to jump with you." She stared into his dark chocolate-colored eyes.

"You will?" His lips curved upward.

"I will."

"When?"

"Whenever."

"As soon as we can?"

Jane nodded. "Definitely."

He wrapped his arms around her, and she prayed a silent prayer of thanks. *Gott* had finally answered her prayers. She nestled her head against his warm shoulder and shivered.

"You're cold." He held her tighter.

"A little."

"I never want to let you go. Never want to let you be far from me again."

That suited Jane.

"The first person we should tell is *Mamm*."

"Let her rest awhile."

"She'll be delighted. She's always dropped hints about you."

Jane giggled. "That's good. I'll have to thank her for that."

Sadie walked out of her bedroom. "What's all the noise?"

They jumped apart and then smiled at one another. Sadie eyed them suspiciously.

"*Mamm*, let's sit down for a minute."

She stared at Jane and Jane couldn't keep the smile from her face.

"Okay, we can sit," Sadie said, hurrying to the couch.

When they were all seated, Matt said, "Jane has agreed to marry me."

"For real this time?"

"*Jah,* for real. This is really happening."

Sadie squealed, jumped up and hurried over to them both and hugged them. "This is the best news I've ever heard. I'm as happy as the day your *vadder* asked me to marry him. You finally came to your senses, Matt. Jane suits you more than any of those other women. I'm so glad you've finally seen that for yourself. Oh, my. There'll be a wedding. Where shall we hold it? Here, or at your *haus,* Matt? Oh, so many decisions, so much planning."

"*Mamm,* why don't we have a cup of hot tea before we make those plans?"

"*Jah,* Matt, *gut* idea. Now, don't talk about one thing until I get back."

Jane supressed a laugh at how excited Sadie was.

Matt leaned toward her and whispered, "And you thought she didn't talk too much."

"I've never seen her like this," Jane replied.

"I'm the last of her *kinner* to get married. I'm sure she came to think she'd never see the day."

"It's nice to see her so happy. I'd feel pretty bad if she was disappointed."

Mr. Grover jumped up onto the couch between them and looked at them both. Then he slowly proceeded to Jane, who was the closest, and curled up in her lap.

"You've found a friend."

"*Jah.* Mr. Grover and I have a special relationship.

We understand each other. I'm sure he thinks that room I'm staying in is his."

"I think it is. It gets the sun in the morning. I often see him lying on the bed in there, stretched out enjoying some rays. I never knew you were a cat lover."

"Neither did I until I came to know Mr. Grover."

CHAPTER 29

IT WAS two days before Christmas Day and the eve of their wedding day when Matt collected Jane from his mother's house for a special surprise.

"Is this a wedding gift?" she asked in the horse and buggy on the way.

"Not really."

"I don't need anything, Matt."

"As long as you've got me you're completely happy, right?" He smiled at her.

"Exactly. It's true."

"Tomorrow will be the best day of my life. No, wait, the day you said yes to me was the best day of my life. So unexpected."

She giggled. "I don't know why. You should've known how I felt about you."

"How could I if you never told me?"

"I guess you're right. We were two pretty dumb people."

"It was all my fault. I was the dumb one. I took my eyes off what was really important. Now I'm going to keep what's important in front of my face, always."

"I'll make certain you do." She couldn't imagine what the present would be. "Is it something small?"

"It's in town at the moment. Stop making me give you clues. I'll give it away and it's meant to be a surprise."

"It's difficult."

He reached over and took hold of her hand. "I'm sure this is a surprise you will like, a lot."

She was definitely surprised twenty minutes later when he pulled up in the parking lot of a large fast food restaurant. "You're going to surprise me with a burger?"

He laughed. "No, not a burger. Come on." He got out and walked over to her side and held out his hand. She stepped out of the buggy and as soon as she did so, she noticed the person in the car next to them open the door.

She thought the occupant would get mad and tell them they shouldn't have parked so close, but then she saw the man's face. He looked familiar. It was her brother, looking every bit the fifteen years older that he would've been.

"Silas!" she screamed and hugged him tight. He laughed and hugged her back.

Then from behind, she felt loving hands wrapped around her waist. She turned to see it was her sister, looking quite a bit older, and shorter than she remembered. "Becky, you're here too. You're both here. Where have you been?"

"I'm sorry we left so suddenly," said Silas, "but we did ask you to come with us. There was nothing there for us in the community."

"It wasn't for us, Jane," Becky said.

"Why didn't you ever contact me?"

"We couldn't. It was too difficult. We had to move on and not look back. The bishop asked us to leave you be when we told him we were going."

"Oh, I didn't know anything about that." She looked over at Matt. "You found them?"

He nodded. "I managed to find them eventually."

"Please don't ask us to come back," Silas said.

"Oh no, I wouldn't. I know you made your choice a long time ago. What are you doing now? Are you both married?"

"We are. I have two children. Eleven and six, both boys," Silas said.

"And I have one. A girl, six-years old."

"I can't believe I'm an aunt and I never knew it.

"And you getting married to Matt. That didn't surprise us at all when we heard."

"It surprised me. I haven't even been living here. I moved to Ohio."

"Sounds like we've got a lot to catch up on."

"We must. Please, stay in touch, won't you?" Jane saw tears in her brother's eyes, and her sister was doing her best to hold hers back.

"We will if you want us to. You must meet our families."

"I'd love that. Would you come to my wedding tomorrow, at least?"

"We will. Matt's already arranged for us to be there."

Matt chuckled. "I thought the shock would be too much for you tomorrow."

"It would've been. So, I'll meet your families tomorrow?"

"You will."

"I have to go," Silas said. "Sorry, but I've only taken a few minutes off work."

"Wait a minute, do you mean you both live around here?"

"Silas does, and I live a forty-minute drive from here."

"I think we've spent too many years apart and probably for no good reason. We can start anew today. We both missed you so much, Jane. We were always talking about you, wondering what you were doing and if you were happy."

"Are you happy, Jane?" asked Becky.

"I was, and I'm even happier now. How about you two?"

They both nodded, and Silas said, "We are."

They both hugged Jane goodbye, and she stood with Matt and watched them leave in separate cars. "I can't believe you found them."

"I had a lot of motivation. I needed to see that happy face."

"You'll always see me wearing a happy face, because you make me happy."

"Good. I hope so."

"*Denke,* Matt."

"Now let's get back to *Mamm's haus* or she'll have a heart attack, she's so worried about everything going smoothly tomorrow. I'm glad we decided to have it at her place. And we've got so many people who've volunteered to stay and help clean after the wedding."

"I can't believe we're getting married on Christmas Eve."

"Well, I promised my *mudder* the best Christmas ever this year. What better Christmas can I give her than to be married to you?"

He leaned forward and kissed her on the cheek, something they never did in public. Jane giggled and looked around. Then she climbed into the buggy. "Let's go."

As Matt started the horse in motion, she couldn't

help thinking about how her life had changed in a few short weeks. She had been in darkness and despair and then *Gott* turned everything around in almost an instant. Sure she'd had a few trials to come through, but they had proved worth it.

As they moved out of the parking lot, Jane said, "You did this for me, Matt, and I'll never forget it." She sighed. "Now I feel my life's complete. I've got my family back and I'm starting a new family with you. This is just exactly what I've always wanted."

"What I've always wanted is to make you happy. That's my job in life."

She smiled. *That* was exactly what she wanted to hear.

"We have *Gott,* we have friends and family, and we have each other."

"You were right, this will be the best Christmas ever."

"Until next year, at least."

FOR JANE, today was her wedding day and the last day of waking up in Sadie's house.

"Are you coming, Jane?" Sadie called out. "We've got an early start today."

"Yep, I'm awake." She jumped out of the bed and patted Mr. Grover who was asleep on the end of the bed. "Mr. Grover, are you going to sleep through my wedding?"

Mr Grover didn't open his eyes, he just changed his position to lay on his back. While she was changing into day clothes to help with the food for the guests, and help with anything else that was needed, she heard the first horse and buggy arrive. Hundreds of guests were expected for the wedding that would start at nine.

A minute later there was a knock on her door. "Can I come in?"

It was Jessica, her best friend and today, her wedding attendant.

"Jah."

She threw open the door holding out a bright blue dress.

"What's that ?"

"Your wedding dress. Lanie made it for you."

Jane opened her mouth in shock. Lanie had left this community to go back with Isaac, only days after they announced they would marry. Since then, she'd heard, Lanie had been staying at Isaac's parents' *haus*. "It's beautiful. She made me that? She doesn't even have my measurements."

"She didn't need them. She's got a good eye."

"That was so kind of her. I can't believe it." She took the dress from Jessica and held it up in the air. "It's so finely sewn and not one stitch out of place."

"She arrived last night with Isaac. Isaac's staying

with the bishop, along with his little girl, and Lanie and Mary-Lee are staying with her mother. They say they're getting married next month."

"I'm so pleased for them. I can't wait to see Rosalee again."

"I've never seen Lanie so happy I can tell you that. She had stars in her eyes. She said the two girls get along so well."

"I knew it. I knew they would. I could tell Isaac and Lanie were suited right from the start."

Jessica sat on the bed. "Enough about them. Today is about you and about Matt."

"Wow. I still can't believe it. I need to help with everything."

"*Nee*. There are enough people to do it all. You should see all the people arriving out there now."

Jane told Jessica about her sister and brother coming. She couldn't wait to see them again, and see their children and spouses.

"Try the dress on," Jessica urged.

Jane giggled. "Okay." She took off the dress she was wearing and pulled the other one over her head. "What do you think?"

"It's beautiful and that color is so nice, so striking with your coloring."

"Ah, it doesn't drown me out does it? Does it make me look sallow?"

"Nee. You look so beautiful. Your eyes almost glow. Wait until Matt sees you."

Jane blew out a nervous deep breath.

"Let's find you some food."

"Okay, but I'll change dresses first so I don't spill anything on this one."

An hour and a half later, all the guests had arrived. It was a chilly winter's morning, but that didn't matter. Matt and the men had erected a large annex off from the house, keeping it warm with large gas heaters. The barn had been cleaned out and cleared out in case the weather suddenly turned bad. When everyone was seated, Jane nervously looked around for Matt. There were so many people, she hadn't even seen him yet.

Then she saw him. He looked so handsome in his black suit, white shirt and black bowtie. He caught her eye and smiled. It took her back to many years ago when they were children. Back then, they only had eyes for one another—never needed to be friends with anyone else. Things had come full circle, just as they were meant.

The bishop motioned for her to come forward. She joined Matt in front of the bishop. He began with a prayer and everyone closed their eyes. Jane was determined to enjoy every single moment of the wedding that she had thought would never take place. She'd never take Matt for granted. She'd always treasure him.

Trevor Mason rose after the bishop's prayer and

sang a hymn in High German. When he was finished the bishop gave a lengthy talk. She felt like the words and the music were washing away all remaining traces of the pain in her heart, filling her with pure joy.

Jane turned her head just slightly and saw her brother and sister with their families. She knew it would've been hard for them to come back to the community for an event, even if it was her wedding. She was grateful for that blessing, too.

When the bishop officially joined them in marriage, Jane felt she finally had somewhere she belonged—in Matt's heart. There, she'd always stay.

Another hymn was sung, and after that, everyone was encouraged to move to one side so the long tables for the food could be moved in.

"We're married, Mrs. Yoder," Matt whispered.

"At long last."

"Finally," he said. "Don't worry, I'll spend every day making it up to you."

"You better."

He laughed. "Speaking of that, I see Lanie over there with Isaac and their two *kinner.*"

"I have to thank Lanie for this dress."

He looked down at it. "It's beautiful, Jane. You're beautiful."

"You think so?"

He whispered, "You're not only the most beautiful

woman I've ever seen, you're the most beautiful sight my eyes have ever seen."

She couldn't help smiling.

"And I can see your brother and sister. I can't wait to meet their families with you."

Together, they went to talk to their guests while they waited for the food tables to be prepared.

CHAPTER 30

Jane woke on Christmas morning, the first morning of their married life together, before Matt. Later, they would join their whole extended family at Sadie's house for a scrumptious dinner. She crept down to the kitchen and cooked a breakfast of ham, eggs, toast and coffee. After she arranged everything on a tray, she carefully carried it all upstairs and opened the bedroom door.

He was awake. He sat there with a red box tied with a white ribbon. "You made us breakfast?"

"I did."

"I should've done that for you."

"Nee," Jane said. "I've always dreamed of looking after you and that's exactly what I'll do." Her gaze fell on the red box once more. "What's that?"

"Just a small gift. You can open it after breakfast."

She set the tray on the bed. "You know me better than that. I can't wait for anything. If this is a gift, I'll be cross. You said we shouldn't get each other Christmas gifts this year. Besides, don't we always wait for Second Christmas for exchanging gifts? Tomorrow?"

"I couldn't help it. You'll understand when you see it." He leaned over and tapped her on the chin. "Don't be cross."

She sat on the bed and took the red box in her hands. Then she pulled on one end of the white ribbon and it untied and fell away from the box. Next she lifted off the lid, having no idea what was inside. At the bottom of the box was a small key. She pulled it out and looked at Matt. "What is it?"

"A key." He offered a mischievous grin.

"I can see that," she said with a laugh, "but what's it to?"

"And, I can see we're not going to eat until you see what this key opens."

"Exactly."

He got out of bed and took hold of her hand. When they were in the hallway, he pointed to the next bedroom. "It unlocks that."

She frowned at him. "You want me to unlock this bedroom?"

"*Jah,* if you want your gift."

She put the key in the lock, then turned it. Was it a

sewing machine, or had he perhaps arranged the room with shelves so she could do her craftwork? When she pushed the door open, it was just how she'd seen the room before. There were no shelves and no sewing machine. She walked further into the room and then she saw it. Curled up on the white and gray quilt was a tiny ball of light gray fluff. A kitten, curled up asleep.

She spun around to look at Matt and he smiled. "Name him what you want. He's yours."

"He's beautiful." She hurried forward to look at him, and he woke up and looked at her with his big blue eyes. When she picked him up, he snuggled into her, and closed his eyes again.

"I knew you'd love him."

"I do."

"Let's eat."

She took the kitten along, back into the bedroom. While they were eating, the kitten woke up when he smelled the ham. Jane broke off little pieces to feed him.

"Now we have a complete family, almost," Jane said.

"Whether we have many *kinner,* or only one or two, I'm fine with whatever *Gott* has for us. All I wanted I now have in you, Jane. *Kinner* will be a bonus."

Jane was pleased to hear that. So many of her youthful years were now behind her. She looked out the window at the dark sky. "I think it might snow today."

"I hope it does. I'd love to have a white Christmas."

She looked at him. "You said you wanted to be married by Christmas, and you are."

"That's what I said, but I didn't tell you who I wanted to be married to."

"I'm so pleased it was me."

"You've always been the only one I could ever see myself with. I only wish I'd told you sooner," he said.

"We can't live our lives with regret."

"You're right. All we can do is appreciate each other more fully now, and be grateful that we're together."

"I can scarcely believe Silas and Becky and their families are stopping by Sadie's after our Christmas dinner. We're all one big happy family now, as much as we can be." Jane giggled.

"What's so funny?"

"I can remember when you told me why you wanted me to come here. Your letter had sounded so urgent. At first, I thought you might propose, but then when you told me the real reason, I was so shocked."

He shook his head. "I should've proposed right then and there."

"You should've. I would've said yes."

"I'm a fool."

"*Jah*, you were once, but not anymore." She looked down at the kitten. "I will call him Sunshine. From now on all my days will be filled with sunshine and happiness. When I look at him, I'll remember how blessed I am. *Gott* saw my unhappiness and He answered my prayers."

"And mine."

He leaned forward and they kissed. When they moved apart, they saw the kitten had seized the moment. He was eating the remaining bits of ham like he hadn't been fed for weeks.

They both laughed.

"Happy Christmas, Mrs. Yoder."

"Happy Christmas to you, too, Mr. Yoder."

IN THE YEARS following their marriage, Jane and Matt went through many changes. They were blessed with three children, all boys, the youngest of whom had his mother's red hair and green eyes. The older two were the image of their father, echoing Matt's chocolate brown eyes and dark hair.

Sadie came to live with them and helped with the children and with the cooking at the bed and breakfast. Reports of Sadie's meals went far and wide, attracting many visitors to stay.

For Jane, life couldn't have been better, made even more special now that she kept in regular contact with her brother and sister and their families. Each Christmas they gathered together to celebrate, and for Jane and Matt Christmas would always be 'their' special time when they counted their blessings, giving extra thanks to God for bringing them together—in spite of themselves.

~

More Christmas novels and novellas by Samantha Price:

(While some of these are in a series, they are all stand-alone reads).

In Time For An Amish Christmas

Amish Widow's Christmas

Amish Christmas Mystery

Amish Girl's Christmas

Thank you for reading Amish Christmas Bride.

So you don't miss out on any of my new releases and special offers, be sure to add your email on the newsletter section of my website.

www.SamanthaPriceAuthor.com

Blessings,

Samantha Price

ALSO BY SAMANTHA PRICE:

AMISH MAIDS TRILOGY

Book 1 His Amish Nanny

Book 2 The Amish Maid's Sweetheart

Book 3 The Amish Deacon's Daughter

AMISH MISFTIS

Book 1 The Amish Girl Who Never Belonged

Book 2 The Amish Spinster

Book 3 The Amish Bishop's Daughter

Book 4 The Amish Single Mother

Book 5 The Temporary Amish Nanny

Book 6 Jeremiah's Daughter

Book 7 My Brother's Keeper

SEVEN AMISH BACHELORS

Book 1 The Amish Bachelor

Book 2 His Amish Romance

Book 3 Joshua's Choice

Book 4 Forbidden Amish Romance

Book 5 The Quiet Amish Bachelor

Book 6 The Determined Amish Bachelor

Book 7 Amish Bachelor's Secret

For a full list of Samantha Price's books visit:

www.SamanthaPriceAuthor.com

ABOUT SAMANTHA PRICE

USA Today Bestselling author, Samantha Price, wrote stories from a young age, but it wasn't until later in life that she took up writing full time. Formally an artist, she exchanged her paintbrush for the computer and, many best-selling book series later, has never looked back.

Samantha is happiest on her computer lost in the world of her characters. She is best known for the Ettie Smith Amish Mysteries series and The Amish Bonnet Sisters series.

www.SamanthaPriceAuthor.com

Samantha loves to hear from her readers. Connect with her at:

samantha@samanthapriceauthor.com
www.facebook.com/SamanthaPriceAuthor
Follow Samantha Price on BookBub
Twitter @ AmishRomance
Instagram - SamanthaPriceAuthor

Printed by Amazon Italia Logistica S.r.l.
Torrazza Piemonte (TO), Italy

13583983R00157